D1104112

Modern Critical Interpretations

Leo Tolstoy's
War and Peace

Modern Critical Interpretations

The Oresteia
Beowulf
The General Prologue to
  The Canterbury Tales
The Pardoner's Tale
The Knight's Tale
The Divine Comedy
Exodus
Genesis
The Gospels
The Iliad
The Book of Job
Volpone
Doctor Faustus
The Revelation of St.
  John the Divine
The Song of Songs
Oedipus Rex
The Aeneid
The Duchess of Malfi
Antony and Cleopatra
As You Like It
Coriolanus
Hamlet
Henry IV, Part I
Henry IV, Part II
Henry V
Julius Caesar
King Lear
Macbeth
Measure for Measure
The Merchant of Venice
A Midsummer Night's
  Dream
Much Ado About
  Nothing
Othello
Richard II
Richard III
The Sonnets
Taming of the Shrew
The Tempest
Twelfth Night
The Winter's Tale
Emma
Mansfield Park
Pride and Prejudice
The Life of Samuel
  Johnson
Moll Flanders
Robinson Crusoe
Tom Jones
The Beggar's Opera
Gray's Elegy
Paradise Lost
The Rape of the Lock
Tristram Shandy
Gulliver's Travels

Evelina
The Marriage of Heaven
  and Hell
Songs of Innocence and
  Experience
Jane Eyre
Wuthering Heights
Don Juan
The Rime of the Ancient
  Mariner
Bleak House
David Copperfield
Hard Times
A Tale of Two Cities
Middlemarch
The Mill on the Floss
Jude the Obscure
The Mayor of
  Casterbridge
The Return of the Native
Tess of the D'Urbervilles
The Odes of Keats
Frankenstein
Vanity Fair
Barchester Towers
The Prelude
The Red Badge of
  Courage
The Scarlet Letter
The Ambassadors
Daisy Miller, The Turn
  of the Screw, and
  Other Tales
The Portrait of a Lady
Billy Budd, Benito Cer-
  eno, Bartleby the Scriv-
  ener, and Other Tales
Moby-Dick
The Tales of Poe
Walden
Adventures of
  Huckleberry Finn
The Life of Frederick
  Douglass
Heart of Darkness
Lord Jim
Nostromo
A Passage to India
Dubliners
A Portrait of the Artist as
  a Young Man
Ulysses
Kim
The Rainbow
Sons and Lovers
Women in Love
1984
Major Barbara

Man and Superman
Pygmalion
St. Joan
The Playboy of the
  Western World
The Importance of Being
  Earnest
Mrs. Dalloway
To the Lighthouse
My Antonia
An American Tragedy
Murder in the Cathedral
The Waste Land
Absalom, Absalom!
Light in August
Sanctuary
The Sound and the Fury
The Great Gatsby
A Farewell to Arms
The Sun Also Rises
Arrowsmith
Lolita
The Iceman Cometh
Long Day's Journey Into
  Night
The Grapes of Wrath
Miss Lonelyhearts
The Glass Menagerie
A Streetcar Named
  Desire
Their Eyes Were
  Watching God
Native Son
Waiting for Godot
Herzog
All My Sons
Death of a Salesman
Gravity's Rainbow
All the King's Men
The Left Hand of
  Darkness
The Brothers Karamazov
Crime and Punishment
Madame Bovary
The Interpretation of
  Dreams
The Castle
The Metamorphosis
The Trial
Man's Fate
The Magic Mountain
Montaigne's Essays
Remembrance of Things
  Past
The Red and the Black
Anna Karenina
War and Peace

These and other titles in preparation

Modern Critical Interpretations

Leo Tolstoy's
War and Peace

Edited and with an introduction by
Harold Bloom
Sterling Professor of the Humanities
Yale University

Chelsea House Publishers ◇ *1988*
NEW YORK ◇ NEW HAVEN ◇ PHILADELPHIA

© 1988 by Chelsea House Publishers, a division
of Chelsea House Educational Communications, Inc.
95 Madison Avenue, New York, NY 10016
345 Whitney Avenue, New Haven, CT 06511
5068B West Chester Pike, Edgemont, PA 19028

Introduction © 1988 by Harold Bloom

Printed and bound in the United States of America

10 9 8 7 6 5 4 3 2 1

∞ The paper used in this publication meets the minimum
requirements of the American National Standard for
Permanence of Paper for Printed Library Materials,
Z39.48-1984.

Library of Congress Cataloging-in-Publication Data
Leo Tolstoy's War and peace.
    (Modern critical interpretations)
    Bibliography: p.
    Includes index.
    Summary: A collection of seven critical essays discussing
Tolstoy's novel, arranged in chronological order of their
original publication.
    1. Tolstoy, Leo, graf, 1828–1910. Voĭna i mir. [1. Tolstoy,
Leo, graf, 1828–1910. War and peace. 2. Russian literature—
History and criticism] I. Bloom, Harold. II. Series.
PG3365.V65L39   1988   891.73'3   87-9249
ISBN 1-55546-078-X (alk. paper)

Contents

Editor's Note / vii

Introduction / 1
    HAROLD BLOOM

"Not a Novel . . .": *War and Peace* / 7
    JOHN BAYLEY

Freedom and Necessity:
A Reconsideration of *War and Peace* / 41
    PAUL DEBRECZENY

The Second Birth of Pierre Bezukhov / 55
    ROBERT LOUIS JACKSON

A Man Speaking to Men:
The Narratives of *War and Peace* / 65
    W. GARETH JONES

War and Peace: The Theoretical Chapters / 87
    EDWARD WASIOLEK

The Recuperative Powers of Memory:
Tolstoy's *War and Peace* / 103
    PATRICIA CARDEN

Forms of Life and Death:
War and Peace / 123
    MARTIN PRICE

Chronology / 131

Contributors / 135

Bibliography / 137

Acknowledgments / 139

Index / 141

Editor's Note

This book brings together a representative selection of the best modern critical interpretations, available in English, of Tolstoy's epic novel *War and Peace*. The critical essays are reprinted here in the chronological order of their original publication. I am grateful to Joyce Bannerjee and Henry Finder for their aid in editing this volume.

My introduction is an appreciation of Tolstoy's extraordinary powers of representation in *War and Peace*. John Bayley begins the chronological sequence of criticism with another appreciation, which delineates some of the ways in which Tolstoy makes *War and Peace* seem not a novel but life itself, so that we read it more than once without believing that we have to perform an act of interpretation.

In Paul Debreczeny's reading, the dialectic of freedom and necessity in Tolstoy produces the mixed genre, novel and epic, that helps give *War and Peace* its uniqueness. Robert Louis Jackson, chronicling the second birth of Pierre, relates it to the creation of Platon Karataev as a kind of Russian icon.

The multiple narratives of *War and Peace* are seen in their intricate balance by W. Gareth Jones, while Edward Wasiolek analyzes the novel's theoretical chapters, Tolstoy's massive meditations upon history.

The doctrine of memory, with its benign workings of the compensatory side of Tolstoy's imagination, is judged by Patricia Carden to be the foundation of *War and Peace*. In this book's final essay, Martin Price traces the very different movements between moral visions, and forms of life, by the novel's protagonists, and concludes that Pierre's change is the one that comes "from the deepest engagement with reality."

Introduction

I

Tolstoy, as befits the writer since Shakespeare who most has the art of the actual, combines in his representational praxis the incompatible powers of the two strongest ancient authors, the poet of the *Iliad* and the original teller of the stories of Abraham, Jacob, Joseph, and Moses in Genesis and Exodus. Perhaps it was because he was closer both to Homer and the Yahwist that Tolstoy was so outrageous a critic of Shakespeare. Surely no other reader of Shakespeare ever has found *Hamlet, Macbeth,* and *King Lear* tedious and offensive. Why Tolstoy could accept the *Iliad*'s morality, and not *Hamlet*'s, is a profound puzzle, since Hamlet has more in common with Joseph or with the David of 2 Samuel than he does with Achilles or Hector. I surmise that Tolstoy, despite himself, owed too much to Shakespearean representation, and could not bear to acknowledge the inevitable debt. Prince Andrew has more of Hotspur than of Lord Byron in him, and even Pierre, in his comic aspects, reflects the Shakespearean rather than the Homeric or biblical naturalism. If your characters change less because of experience than by listening to themselves reflect upon their relation to experience, then you are another heir of Shakespeare's innovations in mimesis, even if you insist passionately that your sense of reality is morally centered while Shakespeare's was not.

Shakespeare and Tolstoy had the Bible rather than the *Iliad* in common, and the Shakespearean drama that most should have offended Tolstoy was *Troilus and Cressida.* Alas, *King Lear* achieved that bad eminence, while only Falstaff, rather surprisingly, convinced Tolstoy. But then the effect of the greatest writers upon one another can be very odd. Writing in 1908, Henry James associated *War and Peace* with Thackeray's *The Newcomes* and Dumas's *The Three Musketeers,* since all these were "large loose baggy monsters, with . . . queer elements of the accidental and the arbitrary." Twenty years

1

earlier, James had a vision of Tolstoy as "a monster harnessed to his great subject—all human life!—as an elephant might be harnessed, for purposes of traction, not to a carriage, but to a coach-house."

James's demand for "an absolutely premeditated art" might seem to collide with Tolstoy's notorious polemic, *What is Art?*, but that is merely an illusion. Even in translation, Tolstoy is clearly a writer who transcends James *as an artist*, even as Homer overgoes Virgil and Shakespeare dwarfs Ben Jonson. The representation of persons in *War and Peace* has the authority and the mastery of what we are compelled to call the real that Tolstoy shares with only a few: Homer, the Bible, Dante, Chaucer, Shakespeare, Cervantes, perhaps Proust. Philip Rahv remarked memorably upon "the critic's euphoria in the Tolstoyan weather." The best word there is "weather." *War and Peace,* like our cosmos, has weather, but no one would want to say that Tolstoy, like the High Romantics or Dostoevsky, had created a heterocosm. You suffer and die, or joy and live, on our earth in Tolstoy, and not in a visionary realm.

The Marxist critic Lukács reluctantly conceded that in certain moments Tolstoy broke through to "a clearly differentiated, concrete and existent world, which, if it could spread out into a totality, would be completely inaccessible to the categories of the novel and would require a new form of artistic creation: the form of the renewed epic." Lukács denied that Tolstoy could accomplish this as a totality, but his ideology made him less than generous towards Tolstoy. A short novel like *Hadji Murad* certainly is such a totality, but the thirteen hundred pages of *War and Peace,* granted the impossibility of an absolute totality at such a length, also gives us "a clearly differentiated, concrete and existent world." Tolstoy does what a nineteenth-century novelist ought not to be able to do: he reveals aspects of our ordinary reality that we could never see if he had not seen them first. Dickens and Balzac render an extraordinary phantasmagoria that we are eager to absorb into reality, but Tolstoy, more like Shakespeare than he could bear to know, persuades us that the imitation of what seems to be essential nature is more than enough.

Shakespeare is inexhaustible to analysis, partly because his rhetorical art is nearly infinite. Tolstoy scarcely yields to analysis at all, because his rhetoric evidently also gives the effect of the natural. You have to brood on the balance of determinism and free will in Tolstoy's personages because he insists that this is your proper work, but you are too carried along by the force of his narrative and the inevitability of his characters' modes of speaking and thinking to question either the structure of plot or the individual images of voice that inhabit the story. If James and Flaubert and

Joyce, the three together, are to be considered archetypes of the novelist, then Tolstoy seems something else, larger and more vital, for which we may lack a name, since Lukács was doubtless correct when he insisted that "the great epic is a form bound to the historical moment," and that moment was neither Tolstoy's nor ours.

II

W. Gareth Jones emphasizes that *War and Peace* is not so much a single narrative related by Tolstoy but a network of many narratives, addressed to us as though each of us were Prince Andrew, receptive and dispassionate. Perhaps that is Andrew's prime function in the novel, to serve as an ideal model for the Tolstoyan reader, even as Pierre perhaps becomes at last the ideal Tolstoyan storyteller. Isaiah Berlin and Martin Price both have illuminated the way that Tolstoy's heroes win through to serenity by coming to accept "the permanent relationships of things and the universal texture of human life," as Berlin phrases it. If that seems not wholly adequate to describe the changed Pierre of book fifteen, the cause is Tolstoy's preternaturally natural strength and not the weakness of his best critics. How can a critic convey either the cognitive wisdom or the restrained yet overwhelming pathos that is manifested in Tolstoy's account of the meeting between Pierre and Natásha at Princess Mary's when Pierre returns to Moscow after his liberation and imprisonment, and subsequent illness and recovery? It is difficult to conceive of an art subtler than Tolstoy exercises in Pierre's realisation that Princess Mary's mourning companion is Natásha, and that he is in love with Natásha:

> In a rather low room lit by one candle sat the princess and with her another person dressed in black. Pierre remembered that the princess always had lady companions, but who they were and what they were like he never knew or remembered. "This must be one of her companions," he thought, glancing at the lady in the black dress.
>
> The princess rose quickly to meet him and held out her hand.
>
> "Yes," she said, looking at his altered face after he had kissed her hand, "so this is how we meet again. He often spoke of you even at the very last," she went on, turning her eyes from Pierre to her companion with a shyness that surprised him for an instant.
>
> "I was so glad to hear of your safety. It was the first piece of good news we had received for a long time."

Again the princess glanced round at her companion with even more uneasiness in her manner and was about to add something, but Pierre interrupted her.

"Just imagine—I knew nothing about him!" said he. "I thought he had been killed. All I know I heard at second hand from others. I only know that he fell in with the Rostóvs. . . . What a strange coincidence!"

Pierre spoke rapidly and with animation. He glanced once at the companion's face, saw her attentive and kindly gaze fixed on him, and, as often happens when one is talking, felt somehow that this companion in the black dress was a good, kind, excellent creature who would not hinder his conversing freely with Princess Mary.

But when he mentioned the Rostóvs, Princess Mary's face expressed still greater embarrassment. She again glanced rapidly from Pierre's face to that of the lady in the black dress and said:

"Do you really not recognize her?"

Pierre looked again at the companion's pale, delicate face with its black eyes and peculiar mouth, and something near to him, long forgotten and more than sweet, looked at him from those attentive eyes.

"But no, it can't be!" he thought. "This stern, thin, pale face that looks so much older! It cannot be she. It merely reminds me of her." But at that moment Princess Mary said, "Natásha!" And with difficulty, effort, and stress, like the opening of a door grown rusty on its hinges, a smile appeared on the face with the attentive eyes, and from that opening door came a breath of fragrance which suffused Pierre with a happiness he had long forgotten and of which he had not even been thinking—especially at that moment. It suffused him, seized him, and enveloped him completely. When she smiled doubt was no longer possible, it was Natásha and he loved her.

Massively simple, direct, realistic, as this is, it is also, in its full context, with the strength of the vast novel behind it, an absolutely premeditated art. Henry James is not one of the great literary critics, despite the idolatry of his admirers. Tolstoy, Dickens, and Walt Whitman bear not the slightest resemblance to what James saw them as being, though the old James repented on the question of Whitman. If the highest art after all catches us unaware, even as we and Pierre together learn the secret and meaning of his life in this central moment, then no novelistic art, not even that of Proust, can surpass Tolstoy's. "Great works of art are only great because they are accessible and comprehensible to everyone." That rugged Tolstoyan principle is certainly supported by this moment, but we cannot forget that Lear and Gloucester conversing, one mad and the other blind, is not accessible and comprehensible to everyone, and touches the limits of art as even Tolstoy does not. It is a sadness that Tolstoy could not or would not accommodate the transcendental and extraordinary in *King Lear, Macbeth,* and *Hamlet,* and yet did not resist the biblical story of Joseph and his brothers, or the strife of Achilles and Hector. The Tolstoyan rejection of Shakespeare may be, however twisted askew, the most formidable tribute that Shakespeare's powers of representation have ever received.

"Not a Novel . . .": *War and Peace*

John Bayley

> *What can be older than the relations of married couples, of parents to children, of children to parents; the relations of men to their fellow-countrymen and to foreigners, to an invasion, to defence, to property, to the land?*
>
> TOLSTOY, *What is Art?*

> *To enjoy a novel we must feel surrounded by it on all sides: it cannot exist as a more or less conspicuous thing among the rest of things.*
>
> ORTEGA Y GASSET

I. FORMS

Most great novels succeed by being absolutely individual. They not only show us a way of looking at the world but make us feel—at least for a time—that this is what the world is really like. At later readings we realise, often with no diminishment of pleasure or admiration, that this is what Sterne or Stendhal or Lawrence see the world as being like. While conceding the truth of what they offer we remain aware of the large area outside them.

In the West this idea of the novel has come to be taken for granted, almost unconsciously. As I suggested [elsewhere], novelists themselves tacitly allow, sometimes even assert, the limitations which their status as novelists require of their view of life. When Stendhal speaks of the novelist as "the mirror in the roadway" he is, one feels, giving in to the *notion* of the novel, recognising its shifting but positive status, as unreservedly as is Henry James in his prefaces, D. H. Lawrence in his comments on the novel's function, or Michel Butor in his programme for an entirely new type of fiction. The newer the fiction, the more revolutionary, the more it uncon-

From *Tolstoy and the Novel.* © 1966 by John Bayley. Viking, 1966.

sciously depends on the novel as an idea; somewhat in the way in which undergraduates in the old days unconsciously revealed by their wish to steal policemen's helmets their acceptance of the status and sanctity of the Force. In the novels of Jean Genet, for instance, do we not recognise the wholly French fictional tradition on which they depend for their novelty and—in Gide's phrase—their *nouvelles chose à dire*?

Although Tolstoy said that he had learnt from Stendhal how to describe war, the *mot* about "the mirror in the roadway" would have meant nothing to him, as neither would that other equally irritating status phrase—"une tranche de vie." Such phrases offer a background to Tolstoy's comment on the unfreedom of those who live under laws of their own making in a western constitutional government. The novelists who invent these phrases, like the M.P.s who pass the laws, are making sticks for their own backs, blinkers for themselves and their fellows. But in Russia there is no obligation to support the idea of the novel, and on at least four occasions Tolstoy observes that this idea has never acquired any real status or meaning in Russian literature. When he makes critical remarks about fiction—and in the course of his life he made a good number—they are seldom about the form of the novel, its constitution and mode of government so to speak, but about the people in it and the man behind it.

"Anyone writing a novel," he says in his essay on Maupassant, "must have a clear and firm idea as to what is good and bad in life." We can press the political parallel further, and say that in the West novelists acquire their individuality, their air of being different from other novelists, precisely *because* they have submitted themselves to laws of their own making, just as the citizens who submit themselves to the laws of a free country are different in opinions, outlook, and so forth. For Tolstoy, difference begins further back, in the heart and in the body.

When the first draft of *War and Peace*, entitled *1805*, began to appear in *The Russian Messenger*, Tolstoy would not allow the editor to call it a novel, although, being almost entirely about family life in high society, it was much more like a conventional novel than the final project turned out to be; and incidentally much more like a first sketch of the ideal novel which Percy Lubbock felt could be separated out of the great mass of *War and Peace*. In the cancelled preface of a later draft, Tolstoy says that what he wrote would not fit into any category "whether novel, short story, poem, or history"; and in the foreword to the first serial version of *1805*, which also remained unused, he says that "in publishing the beginning of my projected work, I do not promise a continuation or conclusion." (We remember that Dickens and Hardy, in their serials, had to invent further instalments and a dénouement, come what might.) "We Russians," he goes on, "generally speaking, do not know how to write novels in the sense in which this genre is understood in Europe." An even more decisive statement of his attitude is the article *Some Words about "War and Peace,"* which appeared in *Russian Archive* after the first three volumes had been published.

> What is *War and Peace*? It is not a novel, even less is it a poem, and still less a historical chronicle. *War and Peace* is what the author wished and was able to express in the form in which it is expressed. Such an announcement of disregard for conventional form in an artistic production might seem presumptuous were it premeditated, and were there not precedents for it. But the history of Russian literature since the time of Pushkin not merely affords many examples of such deviations from European forms, but does not offer a single example of the contrary. From Gogol's *Dead Souls* to Dostoevsky's *House of the Dead,* in the recent period of Russian literature, there is not a single artistic prose work, rising at all above mediocrity, which quite fits into the form of a novel, epic, or story.

As Tolstoy was later to put it to Goldenweiser, "a good work of art can in its entirety be expressed only by itself." Where *War and Peace* is concerned, the question of genre is irrelevant, and it is this that has bothered Western admirers of the novel as a form, both theorists and exponents. "What is *War and Peace* about?" asks Percy Lubbock, who goes on to suggest that Tolstoy was unaware of the fact that he was writing two novels at once. One might as well say that in *Hamlet* Shakespeare did not realise that he was writing a comedy and a tragedy at once. To understand Tolstoy's relation to the novel one must drop all preconceptions about its form, for the Russians make use of that form without adopting it like a constitution and putting themselves under its rule. *War and Peace,* as we shall see, is filled with the conventions, and even the clichés, of the Western novel, but they are never allowed to get out of hand and dictate its development or inform its underlying assumptions.

Henry James could not admit to the citizenship of novelists anyone who would not exercise his electoral rights in the parliament of form, and as a novelist he virtually writes Tolstoy off. But of course he understands very well the issues involved. "Really, universally, relations end nowhere, and the exquisite problem of the artist is eternally but to draw, by a geometry of his own, the circle within which they shall happily *appear* to do so." Relations in *War and Peace* certainly do not stop anywhere, and yet

Tolstoy is not evidently concerned to mount any kind of exquisite geometry on their behalf. So little do the relations of Pierre, with us and with his world, stop, that they may be said never to have started. So many of the important things of his life have taken place outside the action of the book, gigantic though it is. Technically, he has important affinities with a Dostoevskian hero, for instance Prince Myshkin, who also arrives from outside, from Switzerland, with the most formative years of his life behind him and never referred to.

Pierre seems always on the verge of actually living, in contrast with the immense and unconscious life of Natasha, and it is this contrast which gives its extraordinary breadth of reality to *War and Peace* as a macrocosm of human consciousness. For do we not in fact, in life, simultaneously perceive ourselves as living and as not living?—as persons endlessly about to begin, surveying life from the wings, and also as persons fully and physically engaged in the operations of life—cooking, writing letters, making love, and so forth? Consciousness is, so to speak, capable both of more and of less than being alive. And it is this paradox which succeeds in Pierre and Natasha and spells their relation to the rest of the book.

Compare them with some of the most memorable of James's characters—for instance Isabel Archer in *The Portrait of a Lady* or Charlotte Stant in *The Golden Bowl*—and the question of "where relations stop," in James and in Tolstoy becomes clearer. The circle in which they are suspended—the two women—gives them their reality: but if we try to think what would have happened to Isabel on her return to Rome, or to Charlotte in America, we have to give up. James in fact has invoked, and consciously invoked, the dramatic principle: no one is quite real except in relation to the others, and when the circle is completed, then "all smiles stop together." Yet James has tried to have it both ways, like the great artist he is, and nearly succeeded. We *can* think what would have happened to these women and at least to Charlotte—almost he invites us to do so—but only if we are prepared to accept the domination of the dramatic circle. We may think, that is, but we will not think very far; for there is nothing further of crucial importance, of real and continuing interest, to be thought about. In Tolstoy, on the other hand, we feel that after fifteen hundred pages or so he is just starting, when the novel ends, on some very interesting things about Pierre, which he will never tell us about, but which we can continue to speculate on for ourselves.

Among the great Russian novelists Turgenev alone, perhaps, took on the constitutional responsibilities of a Western novelist, and Henry James honours him for it far above Tolstoy. Many of Turgenev's observations about the craft—"I have never started from *ideas* but always from *images*" and "The public does not need you, but you need the public"—might almost have been made by James himself in one of his more candid moments. Turgenev tried to praise Tolstoy by saying that "you are becoming free— free from your own views and prejudices"—free, that is, in the Western novelist's way which Tolstoy detested—detached from life and obedient only to form. Tolstoy retaliated by including Turgenev's *A Sportsman's Sketches*—"the best thing he ever wrote"—in his catalogue of Russian masterpieces that are not novels. The inference is plain. Turgenev is for Tolstoy only a great writer when, like other Russians, he has "created his own form," a form "completely original," not when he is being a "novelist."

II. HISTORIES

Pushkin's tale, *The Captain's Daughter,* which decribes the great rebellion of Pugachev in 1773, during Catherine's reign, is the first imagined relation of an episode from Russian history, but it is no more a historical novel than is *War and Peace*. It strikes us at first as a rather baffling work, with nothing very memorable about it. Tolstoy himself commented, as if uneasily, on its bareness, and observes that writers cannot be so straightforward and simple any more. Certainly Pushkin's way of imagining the past is the very opposite of Tolstoy's. *War and Peace* has a remarkable appearance of simplicity, but this simplicity is the result of an emphasis so uniform and so multitudinous that we sometimes feel that there is nothing left for us to think or to say, and that we cannot notice anything that Tolstoy has not. The simplicity of Tolstoy is overpowering: that of Pushkin is neither enigmatic nor evasive, but rapid and light. He writes about the past as if he were writing a letter home about his recent experiences. The horrors of the rebellion cause him neither to heighten, nor deliberately to lower, his style. And he is just as prepared to "comment" as Tolstoy himself, though he does it through the narrator, who composes the book as a memoir. The Captain, commandant of a fortress in the rebel country, is interrogating a Bashkir.

> The Bashkir crossed the threshold with difficulty (he was wearing fetters) and, taking off his tall cap, stood by the door. I glanced at him and shuddered. I shall never forget that man. He seemed to be over seventy. He had neither nose nor ears. His head was shaven; instead of a beard, a few grey hairs stuck out; he was small, thin and bent, but his narrow eyes still had a gleam in them.

"Aha," said the Commandant, recognising by the terrible marks one of the rebels punished in 1741. "I see you are an old wolf and have been in our snares. Rebelling must be an old game to you, to judge by the look of your head. Come nearer; tell me, who sent you?"

The old Bashkir was silent and gazed at the Commandant with an utterly senseless expression.

"Why don't you speak?" Ivan Kuzmich went on. "Don't you understand Russian? Yulay, ask him in your language who sent him to our fortress."

Yulay repeated Ivan Kuzmich's question in Tartar. But the Bashkir looked at him with the same expression and did not answer a word.

"Very well," the Commandant said. "I will make you speak! Lads, take off his stupid striped gown and streak his back. Mind you do it thoroughly, Yulay!"

Two soldiers began undressing the Bashkir. The unfortunate man's face expressed anxiety. He looked about him like some wild creature caught by children. But when the old man was made to put his hands round the soldier's neck and was lifted off the ground and Yulay brandished the whip, the Bashkir groaned in a weak, imploring voice, and, nodding his head, opened his mouth in which a short stump could be seen instead of a tongue.

When I recall that this happened in my lifetime, and that now I have lived to see the gentle reign of the Emperor Alexander, I cannot but marvel at the rapid progress of enlightenment and the diffusion of humane principles. Young man! If ever my notes fall into your hands, remember that the best and most permanent changes are those due to the softening of manners and morals, and not to any violent upheavals.

It was a shock to all of us.

The tone of the commentary, and the lack of exaggerated horror, are exactly right. In his late story, *Hadji Murad*, Tolstoy has the same unobtrusive brilliance of description, but—too intent on the art that conceals art—he is careful to avoid the commentary, and so he does not achieve the historical naturalness and anonymity of this narrative. He is too careful in a literary way—almost a Western way—to avoid being shocked. The only sentence to which art can be seen to have contributed here is the comparison of the frightened Bashkir to "some wild creature caught by children."

Yet the passage gives us an insight, too, into the reason why all the great nineteenth-century Russians are so good on their history. They feel continuingly in touch with it—horrors and all—in a direct and homely way. They neither romanticise it nor cut themselves off from it, but are soberly thankful (as Shakespeare and the Elizabethans were thankful) if they are spared a repetition in their own time of the same sort of events. Scott subtitled his account of the '45 [1745 Rebellion] " 'Tis Sixty Years Since," and Pushkin was almost exactly the same distance in time from Pugachev, but their attitudes to the rebellion they describe could hardly be more different. Pushkin borrows greatly from Scott. He makes his hero—like Waverley—appear to join the opposite side, and then be accused of treason by his own; and he lifts from *The Heart of Midlothian* the scene in which the captain's daughter goes to the Empress Catherine at Tsarskoe Selo to plead for the hero's life. But he does not borrow Scott's presentation of rebellion as romance, safely situated in the past and hence to be seen—in contrast to the prosaic present—as something delightful and picturesque. Nor does he see the past as something over and done with, and thus the novelist's preserve. Unemphatically placed as it is, the comment of the narrator in the penultimate chapter—"God save us from seeing a Russian revolt, senseless and merciless!"—strikes like a hammerblow. It is a comment out of Shakespeare's histories, not Scott's novels.

Tolstoy also borrows from Scott, in particular from the device of coincidence as used in historical romance ("Great God! Can it really be Sir Hubert, my own father?") without which the enormous wheels of *War and Peace* could hardly continue to revolve. Tolstoy avails himself of coincidence without drawing attention to it. It is a convenience, and not, as it has become in that distinguished descendant of Tolstoy's novel—*Dr. Zhivago*—a quasi-symbolic method. Princess Mary's rescue by Nicholas Rostov, and Pierre's by Dolokhov, are obvious instances, and Tolstoy's easy and natural use of the device makes a satisfying contrast to the expanse of the book, the *versts* that stretch away from us in every direction. It also shows us that the obverse of this boundless geographical space is the narrow dimension of a self-contained class; the rules of *War and Peace,* its *deux cents familles,* are in fact all known to one another (we are told half-way through that Pierre "knew everyone in Moscow and St Petersburg") and meet all over Russia as if at a soirée or a club. Kutuzov and Andrew's father are old comrades in arms; Kutuzov is an admirer of Pierre's wife; and hence Andrew gets the entrée to Austerlitz and Pierre to Borodino—and we with them.

Yet Tolstoy's domestication by coincidence gives us an indication why we have from *The Captain's Daughter* a more authentic feel of history than from *War and Peace*. Pushkin respects history, and is content to study it and to exercise his intelligence upon it: to Tolstoy it represents a kind of personal challenge—it must be attacked, absorbed, taken over. And in *Some Words about "War and Peace"* Tolstoy reveals the two ways in which this takeover of history is to be achieved. First, human characteristics are invariable, and "in those days also people loved, envied, sought truth and virtue, and were carried away by passion"—i.e. all the things I feel were felt by people in the past, and consequently they are all really *me*. Second, "There was the same complex mental and moral life among the upper classes, who were in some instances even more refined than now"—i.e. my own class (which chiefly interests me) and which was even more important then, enjoyed collectively the conviction that I myself do now: that everything stems from and depends upon our own existence. To paraphrase in this way is, of course, unfair, but I am not really misrepresenting Tolstoy. All his historical theories, with their extraordinary interest, authority and illumination, do depend upon these two swift annexatory steps, after which his historical period is at his feet, as Europe was at Napoleon's.

Let us return for a moment to the extract from *The Captain's Daughter* quoted above. The day after the events described, the fortress is taken by Pugachev, and the old Bashkir sits astride the gallows and handles the rope while the Commandant and his lieutenant are hanged. Nothing is said about the Bashkir's sentiments, or whether this was his revenge on the Russian colonial methods the Commandant stood for, and whether it pleased him. The hero, Ensign Grinyov, is himself about to be hanged, but is saved by the intervention of his old servant; he sees the Commandant's wife killed, and finally "having eaten my supper with great relish, went to sleep on a bare floor, exhausted both in mind and body." Next day he observes in passing some rebels pulling off and appropriating the boots of the hanged men.

I have unavoidably given these details more emphasis than they have in the text: the point is that this conveys exactly what the hero's reaction to such events would have been at that time. It is not necessarily Pushkin's reaction, but he has imagined—so lightly and completely that it hardly looks like imagination at all: it is more like Defoe and Richardson than Scott—the reactions of a young man of Grinyov's upbringing, right down to the fervent plea that manners and methods may continue to soften and improve. Now let us take a comparable episode in *War and Peace,* the shooting of the alleged incendiarists by the French in Moscow. Pierre, like Grinyov, is waiting—as he thinks—for execution; and his eye registers with nightmare vividness the appearance and behaviour of the people round him.

He ceases to be any sort of character at all, but is merely a vehicle for the overpowering precision of Tolstoyan detail, and Tolstoy concedes this by saying "he lost the power of thinking and understanding. He could only hear and see." But here Tolstoy is not being quite truthful. Pierre is also to feel an immense and generalised incredulity and horror, which his creator compels the other participants to share. "On the faces of all the Russians, and of the French soldiers and officers without exception, he read the same dismay, horror, and conflict that were in his own heart." Even the fact that he has himself been saved means nothing to him.

> The fifth prisoner, the one next to Pierre, was led away—alone. Pierre did not understand that he was saved, that he and the rest had been brought there only to witness the execution. With evergrowing horror, and no sense of joy or relief, he gazed at what was taking place. The fifth man was the factory lad in the loose cloak. The moment they laid hands on him, he sprang aside in terror and clutched at Pierre. (Pierre shuddered and shook himself free.) The lad was unable to walk. They dragged him along holding him up under the arms, and he screamed. When they got him to the post he grew quiet, as if he had suddenly understood something. Whether he understood that screaming was useless, or whether he thought it incredible that men should kill him, at any rate he took his stand at the post, waiting to be blindfolded like the others, and like a wounded animal looked around him with glittering eyes.
>
> Pierre was no longer able to turn away and close his eyes. His curiosity and agitation, like that of the whole crowd, reached the highest pitch at this fifth murder. Like the others this fifth man seemed calm; he wrapped his loose cloak closer and rubbed one bare foot with the other.
>
> When they began to blindfold him he himself adjusted the knot which hurt the back of his head; then when they propped him against the bloodstained post, he leaned back and, not being comfortable in that position, straightened himself, adjusted his feet, and leaned back again more comfortably. Pierre did not take his eyes from him and did not miss his slightest movement.
>
> Probably a word of command was given and was followed by the reports of eight muskets; but try as he would Pierre could not afterwards remember having heard the slightest sound of the shots. He only saw how the workman suddenly sank down

on the cords that held him, how blood showed itself in two places, how the ropes slackened under the weight of the hanging body, and how the workman sat down, his head hanging unnaturally and one leg bent under him. Pierre ran up to the post. No one hindered him. Pale frightened people were doing something around the workman. The lower jaw of an old Frenchman with a thick moustache trembled as he untied the ropes. The body collapsed. The soldiers dragged it awkwardly from the post and began pushing it into the pit.

They all plainly and certainly knew that they were criminals who must hide the traces of their guilt as quickly as possible.

The concluding comment is not that of a man of the age, but that of Tolstoy himself (it shows, incidentally, how impossible it is to separate Tolstoy the moralist from Tolstoy the novelist at any stage of life) and though the description is one of almost mesmeric horror, yet it is surely somehow not completely moving, or satisfactory. This has nothing to do with the moral comment however. I think the explanation is that it is not seen by a real character, or rather by a character who retains his reality at this moment. It is at such moments that we are aware of Pierre's lack of a body, and of a past—the two things are connected—and we are also aware of Tolstoy's need for such a person, with these assets, at these moments. If any member of the Rostov or Bolkonsky families had been the spectator, the scene would have been very different. It would have been anchored firmly to the whole selfhood of such a spectator, as are the deeds of the guerrillas which Petya hears about in their camp. The sights that Ensign Grinyov saw in the fortress are likewise unobtrusively connected with the sense of him established for us in the first few pages of *The Captain's Daughter:* how when a child on an autumn day he watched his mother making jam with honey while his father read the Court Calendar; how he made a kite out of a map of the world while his French tutor was sleeping off the effects of vodka—and so forth.

The point is that a character like this makes us aware of the necessary multiplicity of human response, of the fact that even at such a scene some of the soldiers and spectators must in the nature of things have been bored, phlegmatic, or actively and enjoyingly curious. But Tolstoy wants to achieve a dramatic and metaphoric *unity* of response, as if we were all absorbed in a tragic spectacle; to reduce the multiplicity of reaction to one sensation—the sensation that he had himself felt on witnessing a public execution in Paris. For this purpose Pierre is his chosen instrument. He never *becomes* Tolstoy, but at these moments his carefully constructed physical self—his corpulence, spectacles, good-natured hang-dog look, etc.—becomes as it were the physical equivalent of Tolstoy's powerful abstract singlemindedness—they are there not to give Pierre a true self, but to persuade us that the truths we are being told are as solid as the flesh, and are identified with it. We find the same sort of physical counterpart of an insistent Tolstoyan point in Karataev's *roundness*. It is one of the strange artificialities of this seemingly so natural book that Tolstoy can juggle with the flesh as with truth and reason, forcing it to conform to the same kind of willed simplicity.

For Pierre's size and corpulence, Karataev's roundness, are not true characteristics of the flesh, the flesh that dominates the life of Tolstoy's novels. The process makes us realise how little a sense of the flesh has to do with description of physical appearance. It is more a question of intuitive and involuntary sympathy. Theoretically, we know much more about the appearance of Pierre and Karataev than about, say, that of Nicholas Rostov and Anatole Kuragin. But it is the latter whom we know in the flesh. And bad characters, like Napoleon and Anatole, retain the sympathy of the flesh. Napoleon, snorting and grunting with pleasure as he is massaged with a brush by his valet; unable to taste the punch on the evening before Borodino because of his cold; above all, at Austerlitz, when "his face wore that special look of confident, self-complacent happiness that one sees on the face of a boy happily in love"—the tone is overtly objective, satirical, even disgusted, but in fact Tolstoy cannot withhold his intuitive sympathy with, and understanding of, the body. Physically we feel as convinced by, and as *comfortable* with, these two, as we feel physically uncommitted with Pierre and Karataev.

> Anatole was not quick-witted, nor ready or eloquent in conversation, but he had the faculty, so invaluable in society, of composure and imperturbable self possession. If a man lacking in self-confidence remains dumb on a first introduction and betrays a consciousness of the impropriety of such silence and an anxiety to find something to say, the effect is bad. But Anatole was dumb, swung his foot, and smilingly examined the Princess's hair. It was evident that he could be silent in this way for a very long time. "If anyone finds this silence inconvenient, let him talk, but I don't want to," he seemed to say.

Inside Anatole, as it were, we "sit with arms akimbo before a table on the corner of which he smilingly and absentmindedly fixed his large and handsome eye"; we feel his sensations at the sight of the pretty Mlle Bourrienne; and when his "large white plump leg" is cut off in the operating tent after Borodino, we seem to feel the pang in our own bodies.

But with Prince Andrew, who is lying wounded in the same tent, we have no bodily communication.

> After the sufferings he had been enduring Prince Andrew enjoyed a blissful feeling such as he had not experienced for a long time. All the best and happiest moments of his life—especially his earliest childhood, when he used to be undressed and put to bed, and when leaning over him his nurse sang him to sleep and he, burying his head in the pillow, felt happy in the mere consciousness of life—returned to his memory, not merely as something past but as something present.

We assent completely, but it is from our own experience, not from our knowledge of Prince Andrew. Like Pierre, he does not have a true body: there is this difference between both of them and the other characters, and it is not a difference we can simply put down to their being aspects of Tolstoy himself. The difference is not total, as we shall see, but it is significant, for no other novel can show such different and apparently incompatible kinds of character living together. It is as if Becky Sharp and David Copperfield, Waverley and Tom Jones and Tristram Shandy, together with Onegin and Julien Sorel, Rousseau's Emile and Voltaire's Candide and Goethe's Wilhelm Meister and many more, were all meeting in the same book, taking part in the same plot, communicating freely with one another. For in addition to drawing on his own unparalleled resources of family and class experience, Tolstoy has borrowed every type of character from every kind of novel: not only does he know a lot of people at firsthand—he has absorbed all the artificial ways of describing them.

Moreover, his genius insensibly persuades us that we do actually in life apprehend people in all these different ways, the ways imagined by each kind of novel, so that we feel that Pierre and Andrew are bound to be seekers and questioners because the one has no past and the other no roots in life, forgetting that Tolstoy has deprived them of these things precisely in order that they should conform to the fictional, bildungsroman, type of the seeker. Andrew is a son from a bildungsroman with a father from a historical novel, from Scott or *The Captain's Daughter*. Old Bolkonsky (who was closely modelled on Tolstoy's own grandfather, together with recollections he had heard about Field-Marshal Kamensky) is entirely accessible to us, as much in what we imagine of his old military days, "in the hot nights of the Crimea," as in what we see of his patriarchal life at Bald Hills. But his son, as does happen in life, is distant. We receive vivid perceptions through him (see the childhood passage) but they remain generalised Tolstoy: they are not connected specifically with him. What was he like as a child at Bald Hills? When did he meet the Little Princess, and how did his courtship of her proceed?

We share this uncertainty about Andrew with Natasha, and—more significantly—with her mother. Embedded in life, the Rostovs cannot really believe that the marriage will take place, any more than they can believe they will die. When Natasha sings, her mother remembers her own youth and reflects that "there was something unnatural and dreadful in this impending marriage of Natasha and Prince Andrew." It is like a marriage of life with death.

III. Deaths

Like Death, Andrew remains a stranger to the Rostovs. They cannot see him as a complete being any more than we can—any more than his own son can on the last page of the novel. He has become a symbolic figure, by insensible stages and without any apparent intention on Tolstoy's part. Natasha fights for his life, as life struggles against death, and when he dies old Count Rostov—that champion of the flesh—has to realise death too, and is never the same again. Not only death is symbolised in him, but dissatisfaction, aspiration, change, all the cravings of the spirit, all the changes that undermine the solid kingdom of the flesh, the ball, the supper, the bedroom. Tolstoy's distrust of the spirit, and of the changes it makes, appears in how he handles Andrew, and how he confines him with the greatest skill and naturalness to a particular *enclave*.

This naturalness conceals Tolstoy's laborious and uncertain construction of Andrew, which is intimately connected with the construction of the whole plot. First he was to have died at Austerlitz. Tolstoy decided to keep him alive, but that it was a risk to do so is shown by the uncertainty and hesitations of the ensuing drafts. His attitude of controlled exasperation towards the Little Princess was originally one of settled rudeness, culminating in a burst of fury when she receives a *billet* from Anatole. His rudeness is that of Lermontov's Pechorin and Pushkin's Onegin; it must have been difficult to head him off from being a figure of that kind. When he first sees Natasha he is bewitched because she is in fancy dress as a boy (an incident later transferred to Nicholas and Sonya) but in another version he takes no notice of her at all. Tolstoy's bother is to avoid nailing down

Andrew with the kinds of *aperçu* he is so good at: he must not be open to the usual Tolstoyan "discoveries." (It would be out of the question, for instance, for Pierre to perceive that Andrew doesn't *really* care about the beauties of nature, as the "I" of *Boyhood* and *Youth* suddenly realises about his great friend and hero Nekhlyudov who is something of a Prince Andrew figure.) Such stages of illumination would be all wrong, as would be any particular aspect of Natasha (fancy dress, etc.) which would reveal something further about him by their attraction for him. Her attraction must be symbolic of life itself.

At last Tolstoy—remembering an experience of his own—hit on the way to convey this. Andrew hears Natasha and Sonya talking together at night as they lean out of the window below his, and in this way her reality— her sense of her family and her happy sense of herself that make up this reality—comes before him in the right abstract and ideal way, in a way that could not have been conveyed by Natasha herself in a direct confrontation with him. Natasha's own reactions presented an equal difficulty. In one version she is made to tell Sonya that Prince Andrew was such a charming creature that she has never seen and could never imagine anyone comparable! This clearly will not do, and neither will another version in which she says she doesn't like him, that "there is something proud, something dry about him." In the final version the magical ball takes over, and removes the need for any coherent comment from her. Indeed, Tolstoy ingeniously increases her reality by this method, implying her readiness for life that can take even the shadowy Prince Andrew in its stride; that is then dashed by the prospect of a year's delay; and finally pours itself helplessly into an infatuation with a "real man" (real both for us and for her)—Anatole Kuragin.

Natasha's mode of love presents a marked contrast with that of Pushkin's Tatiana, so often compared with her as the same type of vital Russian heroine. Natasha's love is generalised, founded on her own sense of herself and—less consciously—on her almost explosive expectancy, her need not to be *wasted*. Onegin, whom Tatiana loves, is like Andrew an unintimate figure, but for quite different reasons. He gets what reality he has from the delighted scrutiny of Pushkin, and the devoted scrutiny of Tatiana. His own consciousness is nothing. As Nabokov observes, "Onegin grows fluid and flaccid as soon as he starts to feel, as soon as he departs from the existence he had acquired from his maker in terms of colourful parody." Significantly, Natasha's love is solipsistic, in herself, typical of Tolstoyan *samodovolnost:* it does not need to know its object, and its object is correspondingly unknowable in terms of objective scrutiny. But when Tatiana sees the marks that Onegin's fingernail has scratched in the margins of his books, and realises that he is nothing but a parody, a creature of intellectual and social fashion—it does not destroy her love for him, it actually increases it! Finding the loved person's underlinings in a book is almost as intimate as watching them asleep. The two heroines are alike in the vigour of their affections, but it is a very different kind of affection for all that. In Onegin, Pushkin presents an *object* for us to enjoy, and for his heroine to love. In Andrew, Tolstoy creates the symbolic figure of a spectator of life, in the presence of whom Natasha can show what life there is in herself.

Andrew is created for death. He looks towards death as something true and real at last; and after all the false starts, alterations and reprieves, he achieves his right end. Of course this is something of a Tolstoyan *post hoc ergo propter hoc,* but it is a fact that all the characters in *War and Peace*— from the greatest to the least—get exactly what their natures require. The book is a massive feat of arbitration, arrived at after countless checks and deliberations: though its huge scale gives an effect of all the random inevitability of life, it also satisfies an ideal. It is an immensely audacious and successful attempt to compel the whole area of living to acknowledge the rule of art, proportion, of what is "right." What Henry James deprecatingly called "a wonderful mass of life" is in fact a highly complex patterning of human fulfilment, an allotment of fates on earth as authoritative as Dante's in the world to come. It is significant that the first drafts of the novel carried the title "All's well that ends well."

In his old age Tolstoy said, "when the characters in novels and stories do what from their spiritual nature they are unable to do, it is a terrible thing." To live, as the novel understands and conveys life, is what Prince Andrew would not have been able to do. It is impossible to imagine him developing a relation with Natasha, or communicating with her as Pierre and Natasha communicate in the last pages of the novel. For him Natasha represents life. It is his destiny as a character to conceptualise what others embody. He perceives through metaphor and symbol, as he sees the great oak tree, apparently bare and dead, coming again into leaf. A much more moving instance of this, to my mind, than the rather grandiloquent image of the oak tree, is his glimpse of the two little girls as he visits the abandoned house at Bald Hills on his retreat with his regiment.

> Two little girls, running out from the hot-house carrying in their skirts plums they had plucked from the trees there, came upon Prince Andrew. On seeing the young master, the elder one, with frightened look, clutched her younger companion by

the hand and hid with her behind a birch tree, not stopping to pick up some green plums they had dropped.

Prince Andrew turned away with startled haste, unwilling to let them see that they had been observed. He was sorry for the pretty frightened little girl, was afraid of looking at her, and yet felt an irresistible desire to do so. A new sensation of comfort and relief came over him when, seeing these girls, he realized the existence of other human interests entirely aloof from his own and just as legitimate as those that occupied him. Evidently these girls passionately desired one thing—to carry away and eat those green plums without being caught—and Prince Andrew shared their wish for the success of their enterprise. He could not resist looking at them once more. Believing their danger past, they sprang from their ambush, and chirruping something in their shrill little voices and holding up their skirts, their bare little sunburnt feet scampered merrily and quickly across the meadow grass.

We can see from this passage exactly why Andrew "loved" Natasha—it resembles the scene where he hears the two of them talking by the window—and why the word "love" in the novel has no meaning of its own apart from the continuous demands and rights of life. He loves the idea of life more than the actuality. When he rejoins his soldiers he finds them splashing about naked in a pond, and he is revolted at the sight of "all that healthy white flesh," doomed to the chances of war. Nor do we ever have a greater sense, by contrast, of what life means, than when Andrew, after all his intimations of death, "the presence of which he had felt continually all his life"—in the clouds above the battlefield of Austerlitz and in the birch-tree field before Borodino—confronts Natasha and the Princes Mary on his deathbed.

In one thin, translucently white hand he held a handkerchief, while with the other he stroked the delicate moustache he had grown, moving his fingers slowly. His eyes gazed at them as they entered.

On seeing his face and meeting his eyes Princess Mary's pace suddenly slackened, she felt her tears dry up and her sobs ceased. She suddenly felt guilty and grew timid on catching the expression of his face and eyes.

"But in what am I to blame?" she asked herself. "Because you are alive and thinking of the living, while I . . . " his cold stern look replied.

In the deep gaze that seemed to look not outwards but inwards there was an almost hostile expression as he slowly regarded his sister and Natasha.

I have suggested that Andrew is not subject to "discoveries," and to Tolstoy's intimate kinds of examination, but this is not entirely true. Tolstoy's genius for character, as comprehensive and apparently involuntary as Shakespeare's, and with far more opportunity for detailed development than Shakespeare has within the limits of a play, could not avoid Andrew's becoming more than a centre of reflection and of symbol. The sheer worldliness of Tolstoy's observation keeps breaking in. We learn, for example, that Andrew befriends Boris, whom he does not much care for, because it gives him an apparently disinterested motive for remaining in touch with the inner ring where preferment is organised and high-level gossip exchanged. And Tolstoy notes that his exasperated criticism of the Russian military leadership both masks and gives an outlet to the tormenting jealousy that he feels about Natasha and Kuragin. But these are perceptions that could relate to someone else: they are not wholly him. What is? I observed that the scene with the two little girls reveals his attitude to life, and so it does; but the deeper and less demonstrated veracity in it is Andrew's *niceness,* a basic quality that we recognise and respond to here, though we have hardly met it before at firsthand. In the same way the deathbed quotation above shows something else about him that we recognise—in spite of the change in him he is still the same man who used to treat the Little Princess with such cold sarcasm. The life he disliked in her he is fond of in his sister and adores in Natasha, but now that it is time to leave it his manner is much the same as of old. Though he has only grown a moustache on his deathbed we seem to recognise that coldly fastidious gesture of stroking it.

> "There, you see how strangely fate has brought us together," said he, breaking the silence and pointing to Natasha. "She looks after me all the time."
>
> Princess Mary heard him and did not understand how he could say such a thing. He, the sensitive, tender Prince Andrew, how could he say that, before her whom he loved and who loved him? Had he expected to live he could not have said those words in that offensively cold tone. If he had not known that he was dying, how could he have failed to pity her and how could he

speak like that in her presence? The only explanation was that
he was indifferent, because something else, much more important, had been revealed to him.

The conversation was cold and disconnected, and continually
broke off.

"Mary came by way of Ryazan," said Natasha.

Prince Andrew did not notice that she called his sister *Mary,*
and only after calling her so in his presence did Natasha notice
it herself.

"Really?" he asked.

"They told her that all Moscow has been burnt down, and
that . . . "

Natasha stopped. It was impossible to talk. It was plain he
was making an effort to listen, but could not do so.

"Yes, they say it's burnt," he said. "It's a great pity," and he
gazed straight before him absently stroking his moustache with
his fingers.

"And so you have met Count Nicholas, Mary?" Prince Andrew suddenly said, evidently wishing to speak pleasantly to
them. "He wrote here that he took a great liking to you," he
went on simply and calmly, evidently unable to understand all
the complex significance his words had for living people.

Apart from the theme of death, the passage is full of the multitudinous
meaning—like the significance of Natasha's use of the name *Mary*—which
has been building up throughout the book. It is checked once by Tolstoy's
remark—"he was indifferent because something else, much more important, had been revealed to him." Certainly Andrew may think so, but
Tolstoy announces the fact with just a shade too much determination: the
surface of almost helpless mastery is disturbed. For where death is concerned, Tolstoy in *War and Peace* was under the spell of Schopenhauer. Life
is a sleep and death an awakening. "An awakening from life came to Prince
Andrew together with his awakening from sleep. And compared to the
duration of life it did not seem to him slower than an awakening from sleep
compared to the duration of a dream." As Shestov points out, the second
sentence comes almost verbatim from *The World as Will and Idea.* In Andrew, Tolstoy has deliberately created the man who fits this conception of
death. With his usual confidence Tolstoy annexes death through Andrew,
to show that it must *be* something because life is so much something. Yet
life and death cannot understand one another.

"Shall I live? What do you think?"

"I am sure of it!—sure!" Natasha almost shouted, taking hold
of both his hands in a passionate movement.

Natasha "almost shouts" her belief because she can do nothing else—she
cannot believe in anything but life. Even when after the last change in
Andrew she sees he is dying, she goes about "with a buoyant step"—a
phrase twice repeated. This has a deep tragic propriety, for the two are
fulfilling their whole natures. Only old Count Rostov is touching. He cries
for himself at Andrew's death, because he "knows he must shortly take the
same terrible step"; and he knows this because his old assurance—his samodovolnost—has gone.

> He had been a brisk, cheerful, self-assured old man, now he
> seemed a pitiful, bewildered person . . . he continually looked
> round as if asking everybody if he was doing the right thing.
> After the destruction of Moscow and of his property, thrown
> out of his accustomed groove, he seemed to have lost the sense
> of his own significance and to feel there was no longer a place
> for him in life.

As Isaiah Berlin points out, Tolstoy's conception of history resembles in
many ways that of Marx, whom he had never heard of at the time he was
writing *War and Peace,* and this applies to his sense of personal history as
well as the history of nations. His imaginative grasp of the individual life
is such that freedom does indeed become the recognition of one's personal
necessity, and "to each according to his needs" is not only the ideal of
society but seems in *War and Peace* the law of life and death.

The rightness of death in *War and Peace*—one might almost say its
good taste—makes a remarkable contrast with *The Death of Ivan Ilyich.* To
Ivan Ilyich's relatives his death is in deplorable taste, and his friends' reaction
to it is that "Ivan Ilyich has made a mess of things—not like you and me."
Why this change? The biographies show us what happened to Tolstoy:
how after the enormous creative effort of *War and Peace* his mind (to borrow
one of his metaphors) went on turning itself round and round like a screw
with a stripped thread. There is nothing surprising about this: it follows
like the night the day. With all his natural genius and his immense advan-
tages—no writer ever had more—Tolstoy had achieved simultaneously his
most prolonged and most sublime imagination of life, and a fulfilment of
his desires in home and marriage which coincided with that imagination.
In spite of studying Greek and beginning to write another historical novel

he could not distract himself from a growing terror of that very fullness of life, that apparent coincidence with all its aspects, which he had attained. It began to suggest to him, as to the hero of *The Memoirs of a Madman,* that death is the only real thing, and death ought not to exist.

Tolstoy had always been fascinated by death, but as a means of analysing and enquiring into life. He used it as a touchstone for evaluating people: their responses to it show what they are like. This is particularly true of his first book, *Childhood.* There the death of the narrator's mother acts almost as a catalyst that precipitates his perceptions about the other members of the household and about himself.

> I felt a kind of enjoyment in knowing I was unhappy, and I tried to stimulate my sense of unhappiness.

At the funeral he is most aware of the discomfort of his clothes, and keeps "stealthily observing all the people who were present."

> My father stood at the head of the coffin. He was as white as a sheet and obviously had difficulty in restraining his tears. His tall figure in a black frock-coat, his pale expressive face, and his movements, graceful and assured as ever when he crossed himself, bowed, touching the floor with his fingers, took a candle from the priest's hand, or approached the coffin, were extremely effective; but, I don't know why, I did not like him being able to show himself off so effectively at that moment.

The same beady eye watches the reactions of the rest of the family. Only two pass the test. One is his mother's old nurse Natalya Savishna—"with clasped hands and eyes raised to heaven she was not weeping but praying"— the other is a five-year-old child, whose reaction at the sight of the corpse is a scream of fear so terrible that the narrator never forgot it.

The little girl's reaction to death is as instinctive as that of Natasha to life. And Natalya Savishna is equally unselfconscious. She tells the narrator that his mother's soul is above their head at that moment waiting to enter heaven, "as though she were relating quite ordinary things which she had seen herself, and concerning which it could never enter anyone's head to doubt." Then the butler comes in to ask for stores which the old woman is reluctant to hand over.

> I was struck by the change from the touching emotion with which she had been speaking to me to this captiousness and concern over petty trifles. . . . Grief had taken such a hold of

her that she did not find it necessary to conceal that she was nevertheless able to attend to everyday matters; she would not even have understood how such an idea could occur to anyone.

Self-conceit is a sentiment entirely incompatible with genuine sorrow, and yet it is so firmly engrafted on human nature that even the most profound sorrow can seldom expel it altogether. Vanity in sorrow expresses itself by a desire to appear either stricken with grief or unhappy or brave; and this ignoble desire which we do not acknowledge but which hardly ever leaves us even in the deepest trouble robs our grief of its strength, dignity and sincerity. But Natalya Savishna was so utterly stricken by her unhappiness that not a single desire lingered in her soul and she went on living only from habit.

Childhood, Boyhood and Youth was one of the nonnovels which Tolstoy singled out as characteristic of the Russian indifference to the form. So was *War and Peace,* and Tolstoy would probably have called *Ivan Ilyich* another. But the early and the late works have much more in common with each other than either has with *War and Peace,* and this emerges most clearly in the use Tolstoy makes of death. In the stories it is an occasion for dogma, because it reveals—as pitilessly as Tolstoy wishes himself to reveal—human egoism, triviality and insincerity. Thus we have in *Childhood* not only the brilliant and sympathetic observation of the old nurse, but also the unmistakably enjoying tone—both Gallic and Olympian—of the commentary. Death is an occasion for vitality. This relish is replaced in *Ivan Ilyich* by the compulsion to confront and outface death itself, but the survivors are to be examined and judged by the same inflexible criterion—are they sincere? In *War and Peace* the question of sincerity does not arise. Death is a solution and a reconciliation, an episode in continuity. It is illuminating to compare the narrator of *Childhood*'s catalogue of the modes of grief observed at his mother's funeral with the account in *War and Peace* of how the Rostov family and Princess Mary respond to Andrew's death. In the first, there is one centre of analysis and judgment: in the second, the crudity of this analysis is softened, dissipated among the survivors, so that we have an exact balance between narration and participation in which judgment by externals no longer applies. This is a clumsy way of conveying our impression that Andrew's death is moving, and that of the young narrator's mother merely interesting. The narrator reveres his old nurse for *not* being interested, but this reverence does not affect the narrative tone.

The bounding vitality of *Childhood* does not of course oppress us as

we are oppressed in *Ivan Ilyich,* but the presence of Tolstoy in it is so
overwhelming that we experience something of the same difficulty in seeing
past him, as it were, to the people he is describing. Indeed the nature of
the work requires that we should not. It is as if we had come to stay with
an acquaintance, who introduces us to his familiar circle so masterfully and
rapidly that we are too dazzled to form any opinion of our own. In *War
and Peace* we seem to belong to the family in our own right.

It is only when Tolstoy subdues himself by plotting an artificial continuity for his characters that he releases our own independent and coherent
response to them. For it is an ironic fact that only by caring enough about
them to invent a story for them does Tolstoy as a writer create "real"—
that is to say fully and fictionally realised—characters. If he does not, they
can only have the static, incoherent, meaningless reality of people we meet
briefly in life. *Childhood, Boyhood and Youth* is full of such meetings. After
his own mother had died, the narrator goes to call on a young friend and
meets his mother.

> My answers to her enquiries about my relations evidently
> aroused her melancholy interest, as if while hearing me she sadly
> recalled happier times. Her son had gone out somewhere. She
> looked at me silently for a minute or two and suddenly burst
> into tears. I sat before her and could not imagine what to say
> or do. She continued to weep without looking at me. At first I
> felt sorry for her, then I wondered whether I ought not to try
> to console her, and how to do it; but finally I became vexed that
> she should place me in such an awkward situation.
>
> "Oh, God! How absurd it is to keep on crying! I loved your
> mother so, we were such friends . . . we . . . and. . . ."
>
> She found her handkerchief, covered her face with it, and
> continued to cry. My position was again an awkward one and
> continued to be so for a good while. I felt vexed and yet sorry
> for her. Her tears seemed sincere, but I thought that she was
> not crying so much about my mother as because she herself was
> not happy now, and things had been much better in those days.

We have an immediate sense of the shrewdness and truth of the narrator's
perception, but neither he nor we are likely to meet the lady again, and so
the perception vanishes, as such things do in life, in a dull feeling of dis-
couragement and discomfort. It is precisely because the thing is so like life
that our interest droops and our curiosity seems futile, even impertinent.
Tolstoy has not the knack, as Chekhov has, of raising the random and the

hapless to the level of art and sharing it with us there. In order to understand people with love, and to present them so that they are thus understood by us, he needs plot on the scale with which he deploys it in *War and Peace,* and he needs to use on the same scale the conventions which the novel has always used.

The method of *Childhood, Boyhood and Youth* has much in common with the method of Tolstoy's first recorded composition, *An Account of Yesterday,* which was to set out exactly what had happened to him for the past twenty-four hours. The conception has remarkable and startling affinities with fictional experiments in our own century. And as with those experiments the chief technical difficulty is the presence of the author, not as a personality but as an impresario and contriver. The conventions of the novel do at least offer an escape route for the author from his art, a ladder by which he can enter and leave his creation at will. There is a great difference between the personality of Tolstoy as it appears in *War and Peace* and *Anna,* and his presence as innovator, analyst and note-taker in *Childhood, Boyhood and Youth.* It is curious that *David Copperfield,* which Tolstoy much admired and which has in its first half so much of the primal vividness of *Childhood,* combines both a novel and also the *Childhood* type of a work *sui generis.* Like Tolstoy, Dickens needed the conventions of the novel; but unlike him he was quite prepared to use them to keep in motion a work which had reached the logical end of its own peculiar being; for with the hero's arrival at his Aunt Betsy Trotwood's house *David Copperfield* as such ends, and a novel with the same title takes over. There is a hesitation, a period of flatness when we say goodbye to David and to the private Dickens with whom he is so closely identified, and then the more characteristic and official vitality of a Dickens novel takes over and begins to absorb and entertain us in a different way. Tolstoy never attempts this peculiarly Dickensian audacity of swapping horses in midstream, but the example of *David Copperfield* shows what a gap exists between the world and the method of *Childhood* and that of *War and Peace*—a gap only insecurely bridged by the transitional attempt of the *The Cossacks,* in which Olenin is a poor substitute for the narrator of *Childhood* since he has not achieved the objectively plotted status of Andrew and Pierre.

Death in *Childhood* is a meaningless catastrophe and an occasion of absorbing interest; it is meaningless because the victim has had no life in the story and only serves the perceptions of the narrator. But when the art of the novel is called in, death becomes part of a plot; and acquires in Tolstoy's handling a natural rightness to go with this artificial one. Such are the deaths of Andrew, of Petya and Karataev, and of Hadji Murad in

Tolstoy's last story. In these there is no Tolstoyan spectator concerned to analyse and to learn from the reactions of the survivors. It is significant that the moving death in *Childhood,* that of the old nurse Natalya Savishna, is not entrusted to the reactions of the narrator but takes place while he is away. Simply told, it is as moving in its mildness as the death of the Virgin in Mantegna's picture. That of the old chieftain, Hadji Murad, is a fine physical achievement, like the climax of a sporting event. Nowhere else does Tolstoy follow the last moments of the dying so attentively and yet with such scrupulous honesty.

> He did not move but still he felt.
> When Hadji Aga, who was the first to reach him, struck him on the head with a large dagger, it seemed to Hadji Murad that someone was striking him with a hammer and he could not understand who was doing it or why. That was his last consciousness of any connection with his body. He felt nothing more and his enemies kicked and hacked at what had no longer anything in common with him.

Nothing, if one comes to think of it, can be more daringly presumptuous on the writer's part than to put himself inside a dying man and describe his last moments of life. Tolstoy does it with Ivan Ilyich as well as with Hadji Murad. But whereas he makes no attempt to explain or to own the latter, the former is his creature entirely. And one of the signs of possession is the determined use of metaphor in his last moments: he is not even allowed to die in his own way. To die is (apparently) to lose the awareness of oneself, and this is what Hadji Murad does, but Tolstoy assumes and retains awareness on Ivan Ilyich's behalf. He is thrust into "the black bag," and "he felt that his agony was due to his being thrust into that black hole and still more to his not being able to get right into it. He was hindered from getting into it by the conviction that his life had been a good one." But at last he fell through the hole, "and there at the bottom was a light."

> What had happened to him was like the sensation one sometimes experiences in a railway carriage where one thinks one is going backwards while one is really going forwards and suddenly becomes aware of the real direction.

As he has done before, Tolstoy alternates the metaphor used for the sensations of the dying with description of what the spectators saw. The account makes a great initial impact, but is not, I think, ultimately moving by Tolstoy's highest standards. We are deeply impressed by our first reading of *Ivan Ilyich,* and our expectations, remaining high, are surely disappointed when we read it again. The description is too weighted, the power too authoritative. But the account of Andrew's death—seen as it is by persons whom we have gradually come to know so well because they are involved in the true and yet artificial continuity of a story—increases its power to move us at each reading. And this in spite of the fact that the process of Andrew's death is so like that of Ivan Ilyich in the telling, and, in so far as this is confident and metaphorical, almost equally unconvincing. Andrew's dream, in which he feels death as a monster forcing its way through a door which he tries in vain to hold shut, is surely a nightmare of the healthy and alive, not of the dying? The dream does not seem his but Tolstoy's; the author's metaphors and figures of speech have the property of removing the individuality of what is happening. Perhaps apprehending this, Tolstoy usually distrusts them, as one feels he would have distrusted Turgenev's graphic metaphor on *On the Eve.*

> Death is like a fisherman who has caught a fish in his net and leaves it for a time in the water. The fish still swims about, but the net surrounds it, and the fisherman will take it when he wishes.

How many of us, as individuals, actually feel ourselves in this position? And it is as individuals, not as metaphors, that we die.

So Andrew dies, but Ivan Ilyich does not. Ivan Ilyich is a very ordinary man. Tolstoy emphasises this continually, but he also emphasises that as a result of his approaching death Ivan Ilyich ceased to be ordinary. And this change is not natural but arbitrary and forced. The background is filled in with pungent and detailed observation in Tolstoy's most effective style— the furniture and decoration of an upper-middle-class flat in the Petersburg of the 1880s is brilliantly described—but it is not affectionate detail, like the description of the Bergs's party in *War and Peace.* That Ivan Ilyich should have his slight but fatal accident when adjusting the folds of the curtain on a stepladder is grimly effective, for interior decoration is perhaps more subject than most human activities to the law which Tolstoy holds here to be typical of all activity except saving one's soul—the law of diminishing returns. When the curtains are adjusted they cease to interest and distract and one must find some other interest and distraction, but Tolstoy ignores the fact that Ivan Ilyich—like most ordinary mortals—is quite capable of finding one. He will not have it that human life, even at its most aimless level, is usually self-renewing. And though we can believe that the sick man would sometimes have hated his wife for being well, he would not have hated her the whole time, "with his whole soul." Sometimes at least he would cling to her as something familiar, human and once physically loved, but Tolstoy became convinced in his later years that what was once physically loved must become for that very reason physically repellent.

It is not so much this, however, nor the implications of the statement that "his life had been most simple, most ordinary, and therefore most terrible" that falsify the tale. No one is more able than Tolstoy to interest and impress us by what he asserts; and there is an almost complete harmony in *War and Peace* between the narrative and didactic sides, as between all the other disparate elements. Nor can we object to Tolstoy's contempt for doctors, a contempt as much in evidence in *War and Peace* and *Anna Karenina* as it is here. No, it is when he imputes all these things to Ivan Ilyich himself that we cease to assent. His death is bound to be painful, but not in this terrible gloating way. In fact, Ivan Ilyich's reaction to his fate has at first the simpleness and naturalness of the great open world of self-conceit which Tolstoy knew so well, the world of *War and Peace* in which solipsism is in reasonable accord with mutuality.

> The syllogism he had learnt from Kiezewetter's Logic: "Caius is a man, men are mortal, therefore Caius is mortal," had always seemed to him correct as applied to Caius, but certainly not as applied to himself. That Caius—man in the abstract—was mortal, was perfectly correct, but he was not Caius, not an abstract man, but a creature quite separate from all others. He had been little Vanya, with a mamma and a papa, with Mitya and Volodya, with the toys, a coachman and a nurse, afterwards with Katenka and with all the joys, griefs, and delights of childhood, boyhood, and youth. What did Caius know of the smell of that striped leather ball Vanya had been so fond of? Had Caius kissed his mother's hand like that, and did the silk of her dress rustle so for Caius? Had he rioted like that at school when the pastry was bad? Had Caius been in love like that? Could Caius preside at a session as he did? "Caius really was mortal, and it was right for him to die; but for me, little Vanya, Ivan Ilych, with all my thoughts and emotions, it's altogether a different matter. It cannot be that I ought to die. That would be too terrible."

We remember Nicholas's sensation at the battle of Schön Grabern. "Can they be coming at me? And why? To kill me? *Me,* whom everyone is so fond of? He remembered his mother's love for him, and his family's, and his friends', and the enemy's intention to kill him seemed impossible." It is this sensation, surely, and not "the conviction that his life has been a good one," that makes death dreadful to Ivan Ilyich? And we know that this sensation would persist until, numbed by physically suffering, he would disappear among such scraps of recollection from his childhood as Tolstoy gives him ("the taste of French plums and how they wrinkle the mouth up")—disappear without other dignity than the right and proper one of being himself. That dignity requires that his death should take place on the same level as "the visitings, the curtains, the sturgeon for dinner," because these were the materials of his life. He is not Prince Andrew. We feel for him as we might for an animal compelled by its master to perform some unnatural trick.

Shestov observed that before Tolstoy's conversion he described life as an enchanted ballroom: after it, as a torture chamber. And Mirsky adds that the first fifty years of his life might be imaged in Natasha going to her first dance and the last thirty by Ivan Ilyich and his black bag. But we are more concerned with what happened to his creations than with what happened to him, and at any time during his writing life he was liable to take over his characters in the interests of some fixed idea. We see it happening in *War and Peace,* with Karataev and Prince Andrew, as we see it happening in early stories like *Strider* and *Polikushka*. Though the process is not so thoroughgoing as with *The Kreutzer Sonata, Resurrection,* or *Ivan Ilyich,* it is essentially the same. But it is easy to forget that Tolstoy is quite capable of choosing *exactly the right person* to carry the message or illustrate the parable, and when this happens we are hardly more aware of the use which is being made of him than if—like Stiva or Denisov—he seemed an entirely free person.

This happens in *Master and Man,* written a few years after *Ivan Ilyich.* Brekhunov, a merchant proud of his ability to drive a hard bargain, sets out by sleigh with his servant Nikita on an urgent business trip. A snowstorm blows up, and the two take refuge with a well-off peasant family. Tolstoy's sensitivity to person and thing was never greater, and the pair of travellers and the family they shelter with appear before us as vividly as do Dron and Alpatych in *War and Peace,* or the merchant who cheats Stiva in *Anna Karenina.* As the pair leave—the merchant being determined to push on—the son of the house guides them on their way, cheerfully shouting quotations from Pushkin's poem *Winter Evening*—

> Storms with darkness hide the sky,
> Snowy circles wheeling wild

which he has read in his school primer. Tolstoy does not bother to give author or title—any Russian reading his story would know the poem by heart. The comedy of this (and Tolstoy's humour, though uncertain and captious, is always something to reckon with) is connected with the fact that his view of poetry—even Pushkin's—was not high. We remember how in *Childhood* the narrator is ashamed to have written a birthday poem for his grandmother in which the form forces him to express what he feels to be insincerities ("why did I write a lie? Of course it is only poetry, but I needn't have done *that*") and how the falsity of the relation between Boris and Julie Karagina is expressed by the album verses they write to one another. The humour here is connected with description and reality: it echoes more subtly the grim and emphatic contrast in *Ivan Ilyich* between the false appearance of life—curtain choosing and sturgeon for dinner— and the real issue of life and death. A poem about a snowstorm is one thing—a snowstorm itself is another: a snowstorm can kill. Yet the contrast is not harshly asserted. Tolstoy also clearly finds it admirable that the young man should have enjoyed and learnt such apt words for what nature is doing. Education increases happiness and self-esteem—those powers that rule over the world of *War and Peace*—and worldly happiness and self-esteem are not rejected here.

> Young Petrushka did not think of danger. He knew the road and the whole district so well, and the lines about "snowy circles wheeling wild" described what was happening so aptly that they made him feel good.

Having shown them the road, he goes back. But the two travellers have soon lost their way again. They are not alarmed, they huddle in their coats (Brekhunov's is much thicker than his servant's) and rest the horse. Tolstoy goes on steadily with detail after detail, none of them particularly frightening. (In his conversations with Goldenweiser he commented on a story by Andreyev that it seemed to be saying hopefully to the reader: "Are you frightened now?—are you frightened now?") Brekhunov thinks about his business, manages to light a cigarette ("he was very glad he had managed to do what he wanted") and finally contrives to read his watch, thinking it must be near dawn. It is ten past twelve. Nikita is asleep. Still not seriously alarmed, but now too restive to remain quiet, Brekhunov manages to mount the horse and makes off to try and find a house. Whether, if he did, he would have come back for Nikita remains an open question—probably not. He feels exasperated with his servant for not having, as he has, something to plan and to live for.

> Suddenly a dark patch showed up in front of him. His heart beat with joy, and he rode towards the object, already seeing in

imagination the walls of village houses. But the dark patch was not stationary, it kept moving; and it was not a village but some tall stalks of wormwood sticking up through the snow on the boundary between two fields, and desperately tossing about under the pressure of the wind which beat it all to one side and whistled through it.

The sight gives him (and us) the first real feeling of terror. He struggles on and again he thinks he sees the village, but it is the same line of wormwood, tormented by the wind. He has gone in a circle. Eventually he finds himself back at the sledge and the sleeping Nikita, who wakes up and groans that he is dying.

Vasili Andreevich stood silent and motionless for half a minute. Then suddenly, with the same resolution with which he used to strike hands when making a good purchase, he took a step back and turning up his sleeves began raking the snow off Nikita and out of the sledge. Having done this he hurriedly undid his girdle, opened out his fur coat, and having pushed Nikita down, lay down on top of him, covering him not only with his fur coat but with the whole of his body, which glowed with warmth. After pushing the skirts of his coat between Nikita and the sides of the sledge, and holding down its hem with his knees, Vasili Andreevich lay like that face down, with his head pressed against the front of the sledge. Here he no longer heard the horse's movements or the whistling of the wind, but only Nikita's breathing. At first and for a long time Nikita lay motionless, then he sighed deeply and moved.

"There, and you say you are dying! Lie still and get warm, that's our way . . . " began Vasili Andreevich.

But to his great surprise he could say no more, for tears came to his eyes and his lower jaw began to quiver rapidly. He stopped speaking and only gulped down the risings in his throat. "Seems I was badly frightened and have gone quite weak," he thought. But this weakness was not only not unpleasant, but gave him a peculiar joy such as he had never felt before.

"That's our way!" he said to himself, experiencing a strange and solemn tenderness. He lay like that for a long time, wiping his eyes on the fur of his coat and tucking under his knee the right skirt, which the wind kept turning up.

But he longed so passionately to tell somebody of his joyful condition that he said: "Nikita!"

"It's comfortable, warm!" came a voice from beneath.

"There, you see, friend, I was going to perish. And you would have been frozen, as I should have. . . . "

But again his jaws began to quiver and his eyes to fill with tears, and he could say no more. . . .

Nikita kept him warm from below, and his fur coats from above. . . .

"No fear, we shan't lose him this time!" he said to himself, referring to his getting the peasant warm with the same boastfulness with which he spoke of his buying and selling.

When they are found the next day, Brekhunov is dead, but Nikita is just alive and recovers. "When he found he was still in this world he was sorry rather than glad, especially when he found that the toes on both his feet were frozen."

This account misses the quiet and methodical accumulation of detail which is such a feature of the tale (the detail in Tolstoy's early story *The Snowstorm* is equally vivid but lacks this method) and I am not sure that *Master and Man* is not the most impressive story, in terms of his own theory of art, which Tolstoy ever wrote. The motives of the merchant, his businesslike vigour and his desire to share his self-satisfaction with someone else, as if it were a bargain; the obvious calculation that in keeping Nikita warm he will keep himself warm too—all this makes the impulse to help the servant both moving and convincing. The moral of the story works without strain because the nature and personality of Brekhunov is fully established and he is allowed to remain true to it throughout.

Mirsky observes that Brekhunov's death, like Ivan Ilyich's, "evokes nothing but the most ultimate horror and anguish," but here he is surely wrong. It is not, after all, the actual death of Ivan Ilyich that evokes these feelings but rather the way he is thrust into it by Tolstoy. One can quote his own words against him—"when characters do what from their spiritual nature they are unable to do, it is a terrible thing." Brekhunov's death, which entirely belongs to him, is not in the least horrifying, but deeply moving and also, in a not at all macabre sense, funny. It makes us want to laugh and cry—a ghastly formula when used deliberately in a blurb or in praise of Russian soulfulness, but here neither more nor less than the truth. In general we feel about Tolstoy's humour that he is not concerned with it himself, and probably rather despises the notion, but that it comes out from under his hand involuntarily when his narrative is at its best.

IV. LIVES

In *Master and Man* we have one of the best small-scale examples of how the narrative is unfolded and given the density which is also typical of *War and Peace*. Closely connected with the way Tolstoy uses character or lets it go free is his use—in the same sense—of detail. He was both censured and admired in his lifetime for the tendency to put in everything about everything, from the grease on the wheel of the cart to the fingernails of the regimental doctor's wife. Turgenev told him that one couldn't really spend ten pages describing what N. N. did with his hand. At their best, Tolstoy's details strike us neither as selected for a particular purpose nor accumulated at random, but as a sign of a vast organism in progress, like the multiplicity of wrinkles on a moving elephant's back. Instead of paralysing narrative they seem only to enlarge its movement. In a sense they do serve a purpose though—they prevent Tolstoy's own purpose becoming too evident. When we see the point, in a limited sense, one of his details, we begin to feel hunted at once. Thus in *Ivan Ilyich* a friend comes in to see the widow after the funeral and sits down on a springy pouffe.

> Praskovya Fedorovna had been on the point of warning him to take another seat, but felt that such a warning was out of keeping with her present condition and so changed her mind. As he sat down on the pouffe Peter Ivanovich recalled how Ivan Ilych had arranged this room and had consulted him regarding this pink cretonne with green leaves. The whole room was full of furniture and knickknacks, and on her way to the sofa the lace of the widow's black shawl caught on the carved edge of the table. Peter Ivanovich rose to detach it, and the springs of the pouffe, relieved of his weight, rose also and gave him a push. The widow began detaching her shawl herself, and Peter Ivanovich again sat down, suppressing the rebellious springs of the pouffe under him. But the widow had not quite freed herself and Peter Ivanovich got up again, and again the pouffe rebelled and even creaked. When this was all over she took out a clean cambric handkerchief and began to weep. The episode with the shawl and the struggle with the pouffe had cooled Peter Ivanovich's emotions and he sat there with a sullen look on his face.

This is not funny but merely determined. Such illustrative intentions are the stock in trade of lesser writers, and it is astonishing that the author of *Childhood,* on the one hand, and of *Master and Man* on the other, should resort to them. But it must be admitted that this uncertainty of touch—

whether deliberate, as when he has the didactic bit between his teeth, or simply inadvertent—is very characteristic of Tolstoy. So vast an organism cannot be expected to have good taste. In the passage which describes the abandoned garden at Bald Hills and the little girls taking the plums, an old peasant is described as sitting on a garden seat "like a fly impassive on the face of a loved one who is dead." It is a simile worthy of a tenth-rate romantic poet or a precocious sixth-form essay. Yet only a few lines later we have the entirely Tolstoyan comparison of the mass of soldiers bathing in the pond to "carp stuffed into a watering-can."

One might contrast both with this characteristically elegant simile of Turgenev at the beginning of *First Love*. "My fancies fluttered round the same images like martins round a bell tower at dawn." This is poetic and charming and we remember it: indeed we already start to remember it, as it were, when we first read it. It seems to promise and contain too much of the plot, not drawing attention to itself unduly, but suggesting that what is to come is already there—fixed and taken care of. And this is in general true of Turgenev's descriptive felicities. They imply that the author is a fixed point, and that the work of art—like a yo-yo—will unroll itself away from him to the length of its string and then coil itself back to him again. Tolstoy is not a fixed point; he is constantly on the move, carrying us with him. His delight in the object in itself, and his copiousness in recording it, is like that of a man in a train who does not want to miss anything as he goes past, carried onward by forces greater than his own sense of words. Railway journeys are always memorable in Tolstoy, like Anna's from Moscow to Petersburg, or the start of Nekhlyudov's journey to Siberia. All his details and perceptions depend on this steady onward movement, which is never arrested throughout his long life.

Most of the tactics and devices to which we take objection—but never the didactic interludes, which are very much a part of the onward flow— seem to be outside this movement, not holding it up but merely extrinsic to it. We do not find such a movement in Dostoevsky, where the patterns are repetitive and dramatically fulfilled. We do find it in D. H. Lawrence, but we often feel with him that there is not enough space in front of us, that we shall soon be going round and round. In front of Tolstoy infinite space seems to extend, and the magical resonance in Russian literature of the troika, the clattering hooves, the onrushing train—all seem to merge into his onward movement. He never joins in the "Whither?" of other Russian writers; he seems to value above all stability, enduringness, the past . . . and yet his progress seems always more massive and more assured than theirs.

Like the current of life itself he is difficult to remember. What was I doing last Thursday week? When did I last see Timokhin? When did the Old Prince first become so fond of Mlle Bourrienne? These seem questions of the same kind. People who have read *War and Peace* more than once, and enjoyed it immensely, can often scarcely remember a thing about it. Yet the same persons can recall the plots of Thackeray and Trollope; what was said by Dickens's characters and what George Eliot said about hers; and every letter and conversation in Jane Austen. Odd questions about the processes of art are raised by the category of great writers we remember, and that of still greater writers we do not. We remember best, perhaps, when we have ourselves to do some interpreting; when the intelligence is fully engaged in the effort of complex appreciation. We remember, in fact, our own powers of perception and sensitivity as much as those of the author. This does not happen with Tolstoy. Enjoyment of *War and Peace* is particularly pure because it is immediate, and no challenge is offered to our talent for modification, for perceiving—as Mill said about Kant—"what poor Tolstoy would be at." As no other author, Tolstoy makes the critic feel how superfluous his office can be.

This then is the chief effect of life in Tolstoy. But the set pieces, the high spots—surely we remember them? If they were complete in themselves we should remember more, but they are never rounded off and presented as moments in time. An abridged version of *War and Peace,* the desirability of which was hinted by critics like Percy Lubbock, would be intolerable. This is not too strong a word, for when Natasha is singing the song at Uncle's, or Nicholas is at the hunt, the essence of idyll pumped into the air is already dangerously strong. Enriched still further it could become overpowering, even sickly. At moments like this we remember how daring is the egoism of the great book, how exclusive in terms of class and privilege. Russia belonged to Tolstoy because Russia belonged, literally, to his class. The possession of the past in which he was so assured is an early equivalent of that enormous, delirious, communal sense of possession which—far more than the revolutionary programme of the Bolshevik leaders—animated the mass of the people in 1917 and ensured the success of the revolution. Tolstoy's instinctive "Russia belongs to me" was ultimately to be echoed by the old worker crying out in the streets with incredulous joy, "All Petrograd, all Russia belong to *me!*" The immense confidence of *War and Peace* depends on the truth of the earlier claim, a truth so explicit and overwhelming that it finally had to give way to the later one. Whatever the defects of the new system, a visit to Russia convinces one that Russians have still not got over the joy of feeling they own their country, as Tolstoy owned his.

Freedom and Necessity:
A Reconsideration of *War and Peace*

Paul Debreczeny

Percy Lubbock was wrong, surely, in claiming that in *War and Peace* Tolstoy had written two novels in one. Rather, as the dialectic of war and peace unfolds in Tolstoy's novel the reader becomes increasingly aware of the essential unity of the private and the public in the Russian author's world. Pierre Bezukhov, who has been the gravitational center of nonmilitary, peaceful endeavors through two-thirds of the novel, comes to Borodino, his huge bulk in civilian clothes cutting an odd figure on the battlefield yet epitomizing the inevitable convergence of the individual and the historical. Subsequently, the French move into Moscow—the very homestead of Russian society—in which Tolstoy's family sagas have developed. And a final synthesis of seemingly antithetic elements—not only structural but philosophical—is achieved in the novel's crucial scene: that of Pierre witnessing the execution of fellow captives and expecting to be executed himself.

This scene—so vividly reminiscent of another mock execution, not fictional but very real, in the history of Russian literature—has as profound an effect on Pierre as the ordeal on Semyonovsky Square had on Dostoevsky. "That hour's experience," Tolstoy comments, "had extinguished in his soul all faith in the perfection of creation, in the human soul, in his own, in the very existence of God." Dostoevsky's hero, Ivan Karamazov, was to couch his despair of divine justice in similar terms some twelve years after the appearance of *War and Peace:* he was to "return his ticket"

From *Papers on Language and Literature: A Journal for Scholars and Critics of Language and Literature* 7, no. 2 (Spring 1971). © 1971 by the Board of Trustees of Southern Illinois University.

to his creator, for he could not envisage an eschatology that could right the wrong done to the innocent. Even as Tolstoy was writing *War and Peace,* Dostoevsky had begun his search for an answer to the problem of human freedom and responsibility, providing, for the time being, merely a theory in a grotesque garb in his *Notes from Underground.*

For both authors the crucial question is: Who is responsible for the atrocities they recount? As Pierre watches the French soldiers going about their bloody duty he asks himself with horror: "Whose doing is it? They are all as much sickened as I am. Whose doing is it then?" Asking this question, Tolstoy unites the private and the social, the individual and the historical in his novel. His groping for a philosophy of history and his analysis of the individual characters are both generated by a desire to find an answer to Pierre's question. Moreover, the question haunted him all his life, and he formulated it even more clearly in *Resurrection.* The hero of that novel, Prince Nekhlyudov, witnesses the march of several hundred convicts from a Moscow prison to the railroad station. The heat, the length and quick pace of the march, and the convicts' run-down state of health—most of them have had no exercise or fresh air for months—cause five of them to die of heart attacks. Nekhlyudov claims they did not just die, they were murdered; but he has difficulty in finding a culprit because the minister of justice ultimately responsible for the proceedings has no idea of what happens in reality and the guards taking the convicts are acting under orders. While Dostoevsky looks for a transcendental answer, Tolstoy blames the social system which exacts greater loyalty toward a bureaucratic order than toward a fellow human being.

Pierre's question is, then, expanded into a novel. During the Napoleonic War, Tolstoy argues, over half a million people were killed. Doubtless, Napoleon alone cannot take the responsibility for all of them, even if he is willing to in his supreme arrogance and lack of conscience. Who, then, was responsible? Could any participants of the war be regarded as free agents? Moral responsibility hinges on freedom of choice; if the latter is lacking, there is clearly no one to blame.

Tolstoy wrote in his article "A Few Words About *War and Peace,*" "Why did millions of people kill each other although it has been well known, from the beginning of time, that killing is both physically and morally wrong? They did it, because it was inevitable, because they had to obey an instinctive, zoological law, the same law that makes bees destroy each other in the fall and makes male animals fight." This was written in 1867 when only two-thirds of *War and Peace* had been published. The final formulation of the problem, given in epilogue 2 to the novel, begins with a similar statement:

If the will of every man were free, i.e., if every man could do exactly as he pleased—history would be a mere series of disconnected accidents. If but one man out of several millions had the power, once in a thousand years, to act freely, i.e., entirely according to his own will, it is clear that, should his free action trangress a single law, laws could no longer exist at all for humanity. If, on the other hand, one and the same law were to govern the acts of all humanity, there could exist no free-will, since the will of all humanity would be subject to that law.

If Tolstoy were to let the matter rest at this, he would remain strictly within the framework of natural science; he would see a causality as overriding in human affairs as in nature. His view of man would hardly differ from that of the scientific positivists of his age: he would regard the human being as a complex organism whose actions are in fact reactions—adjustments to the environment in response to stimuli emanating from the environment. This view of man was indeed gaining wide acceptance in the Russia of the 1850s and 1860s. Ludwig Büchner's *Kraft und Stoff* (1855), which denies the possibility of free will, was the most popular work among the "nihilists" of the young generation—this is the book Arkady Kirsanov recommends to his father as a substitute for Pushkin's poetry in Turgenev's *Fathers and Sons*. Scientific works by Jacob Moleschott, Carl Vogt, and others were widely discussed in the journals of the radical left, such as *The Contemporary* and *Russian Word,* and Darwin's *Origin of Species* appeared in a Russian translation in 1864. Among Russian popularizations of scientific positivism, the best known were N. A. Dobroliubov's essay on "The Organic Development of Man" (1858) and N. G. Chernyshevsky's "The Anthropological Principle in Philosophy" (1860). Some thoughts of the latter essay are actually reiterated in epilogue 2 to *War and Peace.*

As one reads further into the epilogue, however, it becomes clear that Tolstoy is not satisfied with a scientific view: "The problem lies in the fact that, if we look upon man as a subject for study only (whether from the theological, the historical, the ethical, the philosophical or any other point of view), we come upon a general law of necessity to which he, like everything else in existence, is subject; yet if we look upon him also as something representing our own consciousness, we feel that we are free."

Chernyshevsky also spoke of a consciousness of freedom as an illusion, and some students of Tolstoy have interpreted his statement as referring only to an illusion. R. F. Christian writes that "the life of these people [the heroes of *War and Peace*] can be rich, many-sided, apparently self-determined—without the conviction on their part that they are free agents, life would be intolerable—and yet the consciousness of freedom which permeates it can still be an illusion. Men must have this consciousness to live, and through it they live more fully and more richly, but it is ultimately this very consciousness of freedom and not freedom itself which they enjoy." This statement has a relative truth within its context, but it would not satisfy Tolstoy as absolute. If he were able to concede such a limited, empirical view of life, he would qualify to be cast with the foxes by Isaiah Berlin; but in truth he has an urge to be a hedgehog, for the salient hedgehog quality, as Berlin sees it, is an urge to create a coherent moral universe. In a historical process of cut-and-dried causes and effects there is no room for moral judgment; the only difficulty of such a process is that an infinite number of causes may be posited for every event. Moreover, such a dry, objective method of study will not allow for the writing of history from a national point of view. Tolstoy indeed wanted to judge, and he was writing history from a patently Russian point of view, despite all his protestations to the contrary.

For this reason he carries his argument about the subjective consciousness of freedom further in his second epilogue than he did in his earlier note about the novel. Since life is inconceivable without a subjective consciousness of freedom, he argues, and since reason says freedom is impossible, the inevitable conclusion is that freedom as a concept lies beyond the reach of human reason. In other words, he concedes that the concept of freedom does not submit to rational argument. One could not object to this if Tolstoy were now willing to launch into frankly transcendental considerations; but he is not. Instead he applies, from chapter 9 onward in epilogue 2, his admittedly irrational concept of freedom to what purports to be rational argument. He establishes an inverted correlation between knowledge of the circumstances of an event and willingness to allow for an element of freedom in it. He claims a similar relationship between the time that has elapsed since the event and the perception of freedom in it.

This argument has two flaws. One, which I have already mentioned, is that Tolstoy concedes freedom to be an irrational concept, yet he is using it here as if he had succeeded in establishing its rationality. The other objection to his argument is that the amount of knowledge gathered about a particular historical event depends on the abilities of the student of history and is therefore not an objective criterion against which quanta of freedom can be measured.

Tolstoy smuggles in elements of freedom despite his own better judgment, because he is compelled by a propensity to moralize. The contradictions which follow from such theory and practice have been pointed out by critics ever since his own time. Since these contradictions have already been analyzed, there is no need here to enumerate them. A single example will suffice. Tolstoy claims that Napoleon, genius, strategy, tactics, and all, had less to do with the outcome of the military confrontation than his simplest soldier. This much is consistent enough with Tolstoy's general theory; but the question arises: How did it happen that Kutuzov managed to influence the course of events? Tolstoy's answer is that Kutuzov "with his whole Russian being" (rather than with his mere intellect) perceived the inevitable drifting of events in a particular direction, and instead of trying to influence the course of history, he harnessed it. But is an ability to harness history not a mark of genius? Is the full utilization of the geographic properties and natural resources of the Russian land not the best strategy—perhaps not in the formal eighteenth-century sense, but in the sense of modern warfare? It is obvious that Tolstoy longed to glorify Kutuzov and to condemn Napoleon. N. N. Ardens has shown that the shifts of emphasis in Tolstoy's historical views, which one observes as he proceeds from volume to volume of the novel, are due to Tolstoy's increasing awareness of the effect the Russian spirit of self-defense had on the outcome of the war. Battles fought in foreign lands might have been shaped by blind forces, but the defense of Mother Russia was a feat of the people.

Moral judgment is inherent in the portrayal of individual, nonhistorical characters in the novel—the Anna Sherers, Anatole Kuragins, and Boris Trubetskoys get a full measure of the author's disapproval—from which one concludes that the individual persons in *War and Peace* were conceived as possessing moral freedom and responsibility. One would expect that freedom, which according to Tolstoy is a subjective consciousness of the self, would be more evident in the characters' private lives than in historical events. The tenor of criticism has been that Tolstoy's theories serve beautifully in his art proper, i.e., in his character portraiture, but less successfully in his historical depictions. Yet this is not quite so—at least not in relation to the main characters with whom the author sympathizes. What gives the novel viable organic unity is that principles of historical analysis are applied to the portrayal of individual characters, and a sense of freedom informs the depictions of historical events. The application of individual consciousness to historical phenomena results in the glorification of Kutuzov, and the application of historical principles to individual portrayals leads to a sense of necessity in private existence.

N. Chirkov has shown, among other signs all pointing to the unity of the novel, that the fateful stirrings of history—likened to a stormy sea by Tolstoy—are reflected in the turmoil of Natasha's emotional life. When the war is over—the sea is calm—Natasha has also spent her overflowing energies and has settled down to tame domesticity. Albert Cook, having analyzed the sequence of structural units in the novel, comments: "Into this structured time, this process of phases, grow the individual rhythms of the various characters. Each phase subjects to itself the destinies of all. What separates Andrey from Natasha is as much 1812 as the baseness of Anatole; and the titanic force of national events, into which the individual destinies flow, parts Andrey from the Anatole he has desperately been seeking till the moment when, as destiny exacts, he will feel deeply enough to forgive him."

A sense of historical necessity is present in all the private destinies, and above all in that of Prince Andrey. He was one of the last to enter the novel's portrait gallery, and at first Tolstoy intended to leave him to his fate on the battlefield at Austerlitz. "I need a brilliant young man to die at Austerlitz," he wrote in a letter May 3, 1865, to L. I. Volkonskaya. Indeed, the cycle of Andrey's life came to completion at Austerlitz; he had been through love, glory, vanity, and had realized the futility of them all. Yet Tolstoy resurrects him in the same way in which Anna Karenina and Vronsky are resurrected in the later novel. Anna could have died in childbirth, and it was really a miracle that Vronsky did not succeed in his suicide attempt. Both had, as it were, completed their destinies, had come to a realization of their guilt and shallowness over Anna's sickbed, and a deity more merciful than their creator would have let them die. But Tolstoy made them live through another cycle and meet their real, incomparably more horrifying ends. Similarly, Prince Andrey is a plaything in the hands of fate; he has to live again certain painful scenes as if the great sky over Austerlitz were not great enough and as if Napoleon—the epitome of earthly vanity and futility—were not shrunk to small enough proportions.

The story of Prince Andrey's revival is one of ruthless necessity, a mockery of free will. Part 3 of volume 2, in which that story is related, begins with a brief description of the peace between Napoleon and Alexander: Russia has entered into alliance with Napoleon against Austria, and according to various rumors, Napoleon may marry one of Alexander's sisters. The paragraphs giving this information stand out strangely from a chapter otherwise wholly devoted to developments in the characters' private lives, but the passage is not there without reason. These odd political developments, which are patently temporary and out of tune with the general trend of history, are meant to alert the reader to the strange, zigzagging path of life. They warn that the new turns the characters encounter in their destinies may be as treacherous and temporary as those in the destiny of the nation.

There follows the description of Andrey's journey to Otradnoe and of his famous encounter with an old oak. As he identifies with the tree, the reader comes to understand that Andrey is as subject to nature's immutable laws as any vegetation. Significantly, his first meeting with Natasha, as he rides up to the Rostovs' house, is an encounter with the symbol of a young girl rather than with a real person; one is never told, he merely assumes, that the slim girl in the yellow dress is really Natasha. She is not important as a person; what is important is Andrey's reaction to a young creature to whom—he painfully realizes—he means nothing and with whom he feels like a hardened relic of the past, like the oak among the young birches. In one of his early drafts Tolstoy intended to let Andrey be swept off his feet by Natasha; in another version he would have been irritated by her. The former draft also shows hesitation as to how Natasha should react to the prince: both a favorable and an adverse reaction are struck out from the same page. I think Tolstoy came to the eventual solution—having Andrey intrigued but not infatuated and dispensing with Natasha's reaction—because he wanted to underscore the impersonality of Andrey's feelings. Although the reader assumes that Andrey has been introduced to her, he is not seen actually face to face with Natasha; and the most important scene occurs when he is a chance witness to her conversation with Sonya at night—a scene in which Tolstoy, once more, does not say definitely to whom the voices belong. The impression thus created is that Andrey's feelings have been aroused, not by a person, but by a faceless feminine image. When the old oak, all green and sprouting, reappears, the sense of a biological, rather than psychological and individual, rejuvenation is reinforced. And to drive the message home entirely, Tolstoy comments that Andrey has begun casting around for reasons to go to St. Petersburg. With his intellect, he should know that another marriage would only lead to a painful repetition of his relations to Lise and that public life is a Vanity Fair; yet he goes because the restlessness of spring drives him—a force in the face of which he can use his intellect only for rationalizations.

It is very likely that Tolstoy had Prince Andrey in mind when he wrote in epilogue 2: "However often reflection and experience may show a man that, given the same conditions and character, he will always, at a given juncture, do precisely what he did before, he will none the less feel assured that he can act as he pleases even though he may be engaging for the thousandth time in action which has hitherto always ended in the same way."

Prince Andrey, like the hypothetical man of this passage, faces familiar circumstances when he decides to reenter life, and not only because of his marriage to Lise and the vainglorious Austrian campaign but also because, close as he is to his father, his father's experiences are in a sense his own. At the beginning of the novel, when he tells his father he has decided to go off to war despite his wife's pregnancy, the old prince welcomes his resoluteness. It is implied that the old man knows the futility of marital relations all too well; he does not even have to be told the full story. Father and son are so much alike that they go through similar and interlocking cycles. When Andrey, vital and energetic, goes off to war, the old Bolkonsky, like a hermit, holds fast to his embittered seclusion; but a year or so later, when Andrey has become the recluse of Bogucharovo, his father bounces back to life, busying himself with the organization of the local militia. Like father, like son—Andrey should draw on his father's experiences as much as on his own. In this sense, he is facing the snares of life, figuratively, for the thousandth time, like the hypothetical man of the epilogue. But there the similarity between him and the latter ends. While the man of the epilogue decides to act out of a consciousness of freedom, Andrey is pushed into action by nature's inevitable forces. Spring has reawakened vitality in him as it does in the old oak.

Necessity permeates the lives of the other main characters too. As he marches with the prisoners of war, Pierre reflects on his past and decides that his marriage to Hélène was not voluntary. And further, his conversion to freemasonry furnishes a classic example of the way in which a man's spiritual energies come to terminal exhaustion under the weight of an unsuccessful marriage and a successful duel—this latter, an act inexpressibly repulsive to him in its violence.

The theme of necessity recurs even in scenes which, by right, should bear the message of freedom. Natasha's decision to elope with Anatole Kuragin is a moral choice, yet it is emphasized that she could not help it. Anatole's presence mesmerizes her, she feels no moral barrier between him and herself, she is drawn to him by a magnetic force. She refuses to understand that her choice of Anatole means the loss of Andrey; in fact she refuses to choose altogether. Sonya's remonstrances surprise her unpleasantly and she wonders how her confidante could fail to see that there is no choice. Finally, the outcome of the affair testifies to the decisive influence of her environment, for she lives among people who will not allow her to ruin her life.

The most "existential" situation in the novel occurs on the "last day of Moscow." The Rostovs have loaded all their valuable belongings on carts and are ready to take flight from the city. At this moment wounded officers begin begging the Rostovs to make room for them on the carts. As the number of wounded who want to come rapidly multiplies, the Rostovs face a choice between carrying along their belongings and their fellow countrymen, between self-interest and charity. To be sure, Tolstoy wishes to say that these are Russian patriots, capable of making the right choice. Yet the theme of necessity surfaces even in this scene. Count Rostov gives orders, at first, to make room for only a couple of people, and even those orders he mutters half-heartedly as if he were caught up in an embarrassing social situation rather than one requiring a major moral decision. He does not realize he is making a major decision until the affair nearly overwhelms him and he has to explain it to his wife. And when the decision has been made and the servants are unloading the carts to accommodate the wounded, the inevitability of this course of action is reemphasized: "When she [Natasha] gave the order to unload the vehicles the servants could not believe their ears; they gathered round her and would not do it till the count told them that it was by their mistress's desire. Then they were no less convinced of the impossibility of leaving the wounded than they had been, a few minutes before, of the necessity of carrying away all the property, and they set to work with a will." The implication is that, given their characters as the servants know them, the Rostovs could not have acted otherwise.

Tolstoy's depiction of history, although its guiding principle is claimed to be a theory of necessity, gravitates nevertheless toward expressions of free will and reasserts moral values. Conversely, his characters, who should in theory be the main vehicles of individual moral freedom, tend actually to be clad in iron necessity.

The concept of freedom is necessary to *War and Peace* because without it neither foreign invaders nor Frenchified Russians could be adjudged. But the theory of freedom, as expressed in epilogue 2, is not carried over into practice when characters close to Tolstoy's heart are portrayed. Prince Andrey, for example, came out of his seclusion, not with a consciousness of freedom, but because he had been rejuvenated simply by biological forces. If one examines a reverse process in his life—the process of his gradual withdrawal from existence after the battle of Borodino—the conclusion seems inescapable that the problem of freedom is, once more, scarcely relevant.

It might be argued that Andrey's withdrawal from life means a victory of necessity over freedom. He has realized the vainglory of the military existence and the futility of the statesman's reforms: he wishes to have no part of either. He has been through love's treacherous plots twice, and instead of love of woman he gives himself over to love of mankind—a condition that for Tolstoy means love of no one in particular and signifies lack of life. His realization of how life's forces work has enabled him to rise above life. Life has become for him all cause and effect, clear but totally alien. As John Bayley writes, "it is his destiny to conceptualise what others embody." He can watch his own destiny in as detached a manner as if he were reading a history book. But history is all necessity, all causality; the element of freedom departs from it as soon as the subject's participation ceases.

If this view of Andrey were true, its truth would be relevant to the process in the reversed direction, which is to say that Andrey would have been revitalized in 1809 by an increased awareness of freedom. But that was not the case; on the contrary, Andrey lost rational control over his actions and was driven by an instinctive force. What Tolstoy must here be referring to, then—at least in practice if not in theory—is vitality rather than freedom. When the great globe of sky opens up above Andrey, and Napoleon shrinks to toy size, the change brought about is not the loss of freedom but the loss of a sense of importance in earthly things. It is not that there are no further choices open to him, but rather that whatever he chooses, it will not matter. From a bird's-eye view the destruction of half a million people may be like a fairy tale; from the detached perspective Andrey acquires in the last phase of his illness, it makes no difference that he is leaving an orphan behind. To participate in life, one must feel that life is important. The lack of this sense of importance is the lack of vitality. To put it in Chernyshevsky's terms, the organism that loses its ability to respond to stimuli—to feel the importance of stimuli, so to speak—is no longer viable. Tolstoy does not prove in his novel that the sensation of life is a consciousness of freedom. Instead, wittingly or unwittingly, he shows that those who exercise their muscles—fight for their country, prepare to elope, chase wolves, go to balls, marry, and multiply—are alive; in other words, the sensation of life is the feeling that one is reacting to the environment, flexibly adjusting to its complex demands.

Andrey's responses grow limp because of a physical cause, his fatal wound. But the somatic process is paralleled by the psychological one of opting out of life. Although this psychological process is brought on by the somatic cause, its components have been present, in a hidden or less developed form, in Andrey's personality before he is wounded. His main traits, as Frank F. Seeley has analyzed them, are a tremendous pride and an equally strong diffidence, leading to disdain. An example Seeley refers to is Andrey's reception at the Austrian Court: "He had been sent post-haste from Krems by Kutuzov to report the reverse inflicted on the French and arrived glowing with patriotic and personal satisfaction, to be received with a polite lack of enthusiasm which cut him to the quick. . . . The coolness of his reception hurts Andrey both in his pride and in his feelings. But instead of reacting with disappointment, which would put him in a position of inferiority, or with anger, which would admit the offenders to be his equals, he avoids the issue and sublimates his pain by withdrawing to a position of assumed superiority."

This well-taken observation is relevant to many other situations in Andrey's life. For instance, when he obviously fails to achieve sexual harmony with his wife, his reaction is to scorn all women rather than to admit his failure or to direct his anger at Lise. If something hurts him, he does not attempt to remove the cause of the pain but tells himself that the cause is so contemptible it cannot possibly bring pain. Natasha's infidelity is an even greater wound to his ego than is his unhappy marriage, yet his main reaction is disdain, a contempt for himself for having ever trusted her. Letting things hurt, refusing to adjust to his environment, disclaiming his emotions—these are the means whereby Andrey opts out of life psychologically. The last phase of this process sets in after he talks with Natasha:

> "Natasha, I love you too much; I love you more than all the world."
>
> "And I—" she looked away an instant. "Why too much?" she asked.
>
> "Why too much? Tell me, from the bottom of your heart, what you think: Shall I live?"
>
> "I am sure of it—sure of it!" cried Natasha, seizing his hands with growing excitment. He did not reply.
>
> "How good that would be!" he sighed, and he kissed her hand.

At first sight, this dialogue hardly reveals the causes that bring on "that thing" as Natasha calls it in bewilderment—the last phase of his withdrawal from life. Yet the elements that comprise the process are subtly there. When he says he loves her "too much" he means that his love is greater than she can ever return, particularly in view of her previous infidelity. She understands the reproach and looks away for an instant, breaking off her reply, guilty. The next moment she comes back with the question: "Why too much?" as if wishing to challenge him to remonstrate aloud, to bring complaints into the open and give her an opportunity to apologize, affirming the greatness of her love. Here is an opportunity for Andrey to respond to a challenge, to clarify and happily resolve the only vital problem which still ties him to life and through which he might be able to reenter life. He hesitates a moment, repeating her question. Then he answers, like a Chekhov character, with an apparently irrelevant question of his own. But in fact he implies that he will probably die, which means he is unwilling to take up the challenge. He would love Natasha as much as life; but he is no longer able to love life. Even the most powerful stimulus—a sincere offer of love from the woman who has meant so much to him—is unable to elicit a response from him.

The quality Andrey gradually loses—vitality—is abundant in Natasha, Nikolay Rostov, Platon Karataev, and others—all curiously unintellectual people. Andrey, the intellectual soldier, is doomed; Pierre, another thinker and seeker, is saved only because his energies are recharged out of Platon's and Natasha's inexhaustible resources of vitality. The intellect is suspect, ineffectual, devoid of life. This idea of Tolstoy's became crystallized a decade later in *A Confession:* "Rational knowledge does not give the meaning of life, but excludes life; while the meaning attributed to life by millions of people, by all humanity, rests on some despised pseudo-knowledge."

Although *War and Peace* was written with polemic intent against *La Paix et la Guerre,* Proudhon's anti-intellectualism looms large in it. Certain currents of Russian culture of the second half of the century also reinforce Tolstoy's rejection of intellectualism: slavophilism and populism both conjured up deep-seated emotional forces; for Dostoevsky, intellect was the dwelling place of evil; and Turgenev portrayed the ineffectual Rudin in the framework of a Hamlet-Don Quixote opposition to Insarov.

The anti-intellectual features of *War and Peace* have, moreover, a certain connection with its epic qualities. Both George Lukács and George Steiner have argued its affinity to the ancient epic, particularly to *The Iliad.* Both emphasize the importance of a unified world view which sees objects and people, people and leaders as one organic whole. One of the features of the epic that Steiner lists seems to be especially relevant: "The recognition that energy and aliveness are, of themselves, holy."

The "wholeness" of life is the quality of a patriarchal *ancien régime.* Tolstoy lived in an age when this patriarchal order was being threatened by the advance of an industrialized society, a society in which, as R. P. Blackmur has argued, the problem is not the individual's conflict with the existing moral order, but his need to establish a moral universe for himself since society's former uniform values have crumbled. Western rationalism, advancing natural sciences, these were the torchbearers in Tolstoy's eyes of this approaching new society, and its hallmark was chaos. In a last-ditch effort to save the secure, comprehensive unity of his world, he attacked the intellect on two fronts. On the one hand, he tried to deny it freedom and effectiveness: military leaders, he argued, only imagine they can win battles by clever strategies; historians who try to explain the causes of events err hopelessly; and so forth. He suspected that the intellect, if it penetrated too far, would open up vistas impossible of integration; alienation would inevitably result. On the other hand, the denial of freedom of action and the establishment of strict causality were precisely the results that modern empirical science was offering on an unprecedented scale. For this reason Tolstoy came to reaffirm freedom on an irrational basis, either unable to comprehend or unwilling to accept that consciousness contemplating itself in its full complexity—what he called the consciousness of freedom—could still be subject to the laws of nature. The tension between Tolstoy's contradictory ideas on freedom and necessity produced the mixed genre—half epic, half novel—that is *War and Peace*.

The Second Birth of Pierre Bezukhov

Robert Louis Jackson

> *For I cannot otherwise reach the Kingdom of Heaven unless I am born a second time. Therefore I desire to return to the mother's womb, that I may be regenerated, and this I will do right soon.*
> GEORG VON WELLING, *Opus Mago-Cabbalisticum et Theosiphicum* (1735)

Pierre's experience in Moscow after the battle of Borodino is pivotal in his development: he moves from a state of extreme individualism and psychological imbalance to an almost complete loss of identity and spiritual collapse. The whole experience from his meeting with Ramballe to his witnessing of the executions on Devichii Field is traumatic for him. His meeting with Platon Karataev after the executions signals his psychological and spiritual recovery and the beginning of a new phase in his life. Tolstoy's presentation of Pierre's meeting with Platon—his understanding of the process of recovery—deserves close attention.

The executions that Pierre witnesses on Devichii Field bring him to near spiritual death—a sense of total void. (*Devichii*—girlish, maidenly. In a sense one may say that Pierre definitively loses all innocent view of the world on this "virgin" field.) The central question of his own identity is posed at the time of his arrest during the interrogations: "Who is he? Where had he come from?—With what purpose, etc." His crisis of identity is accompanied by a terrifying impression of the irrationality and senselessness of the processes taking charge of his life. Who, he wonders, has condemned him? "Who, then, finally, was executing him, killing him, taking his life— his, Pierre's, with all his memories, aspirations, hopes and thoughts? Who

From *Canadian-American Slavic Studies* 12, no. 4 (Winter 1978). © 1978 by Charles Schlacks, Jr., and Arizona State University.

was doing this? And Pierre felt that it was no one [*nikto*]. It was the system, the concatenation of circumstances. Some kind of system was killing him, Pierre, depriving him of life, everything, annihilating him." Nikto is the messenger of death on Devichii Field. Pierre's last hold on moral reality is shattered by the execution scene. Reprieved, but cruelly not informed of the act of judicial mercy—the special dispensation of General Davout—he is marched to the place of execution with other prisoners condemned as incendiaries. He walks, mechanically, in a state of complete moral and mental stupefaction. He can neither think nor reflect; he only hears and sees. The horror of death and the sense of the absurd overpower him as he watches, finally, earth being shovelled onto an executed but still dying man.

Tolstoy sums up Pierre's condition after the executions:

> From the moment Pierre witnessed those horrifying murders committed by people who had no wish to commit them, it was as if the mainspring of his soul which held everything together and which made everything seem alive were pulled out, and everything collapsed into a heap of meaningless rubbish. Though he was not even aware of it, his faith in a well-ordered universe [*v blagoustroistvo mira*], in humanity, in his own soul, in God, had been destroyed. Pierre had experienced this before but never with such intensity as now. Formerly when doubts of this sort had come upon him the doubts had arisen from his own fault [*vina*]. And in the depths of his soul Pierre in those times had felt that salvation from that despair and those doubts was to be found within himself. But now he felt that it was through no fault of his own that the universe had crumbled before his eyes and only meaningless ruins remained. He felt that it was not in his power to regain his faith in life.

This description of Pierre's spiritual crisis occurs in the third paragraph of the chapter centering on his encounter with the Russian peasant, Platon Karataev; the scene is set in the darkness of one of the sheds where prisoners were gathered. The sense of almost irremediable spiritual devastation, however, is foreshadowed in the opening lines of the chapter. "After the executions Pierre was separated from the other prisoners and left by himself in *a small, ruined and befouled church*"; here he is informed by two French soldiers of his reprieve and thence taken to a shed "made of *charred planks, beams and battens* (my italics). Tolstoy's play upon the word "reprieved" (*proshchen*, literally, "forgiven") subtly contributes to our understanding of Pierre's moral and spiritual stupefaction: in a desecrated church he is given" by the new military authorities—the representatives of the Antichrist Napoleon—for a crime of which he is not guilty; he is forgiven at a moment when he can in no way connect his sense of inner spiritual collapse and chaos with any sense of personal guilt or blame. The objective irony of the situation is reflected in Pierre's sense of the absurd.

His subjective confusion, then, reflects the irrationality and disfiguration of things and relations in a world which has lost all those "connections" that are part of a functioning social structure. Utterly shattered, he follows the soldiers to a shed (*balagan*) "without understanding what they said to him." (*Balagan*—a booth, stall or stand [as at fairs]; a temporary wooden structure, etc.; also, in folk theatre, a low farce.) Once inside the shed he looks at the people in the darkness around him "without understanding who these people were." He hears words but draws no inference from them, finds them irrelevant: "he did not understand their significance." He answers questions mechanically. "He looked at their faces and figures and they all seemed to him equally senseless."

Tolstoy stresses not only the spiritual anomie of Pierre but his physical helplessness. "People . . . led [*him*] somewhere and at last he found himself in a corner of the shed." His mental and physical state seems almost to resemble that of an infant. "Sitting silently and motionlessly on the straw near the wall Pierre now opened, now closed his eyes." But what he sees when he closes them are the terrible scenes of the executions. "And once again he opened his eyes and stared senselessly into the darkness."

It is in this state of almost complete physical and mental prostration that Pierre becomes aware of a "little man" sitting near him and looking at him. His awakening, or return to normal consciousness, begins at this point. The process as Tolstoy conceives it is entirely organic; instinctual rather than cerebral or conceptual, Pierre's return to life involves first of all the senses: smell, sight, sound, taste and even touch. His awakening begins with the stimulation of the most primitive sense: *smell*. Just as an infant recognizes its mother by its sense of smell, so Pierre first notices Platon Karataev—on the symbolic plane a very distinct mother surrogate for him—"by a strong smell of sweat." Next, he is stimulated by *sight*: his interest is aroused—indeed there is something childlike in his curiosity— by certain circular movements: Platon is unwinding the bands around his footgear. "Pierre was conscious of something pleasant, soothing and complete in those deft movements, in the man's well-ordered arrangements [*v etom blagoustroennom . . . khoziaistve*] in his corner, even the very smell of the man, and he could not take his eyes off him." Pierre—Tolstoy had noted but a moment before—had lost his faith "in a well-ordered universe

[*v blagoustroistvo mira*], in humanity, in his own soul, in God." The restoration of Pierre's well-ordered universe—that spiritual macrocosm with its
grand and harmonious orbital movements—begins with the "well-ordered
. . . arrangements" of Platon, the circular movements of the little world
or microcosm. Tolstoy's thought is clear: our sense of life as something
meaningful, our values, at once ethical and aesthetic, find their source in
the concrete fundamentals of living, the basic needs, patterns and rhythms
of life. The sense of life's meaning is not to be found in a set of abstract
concepts or propositions, but in the concrete processes of the "living life"
and in man's organic participation in them.

Pierre's spiritual regeneration, then, begins with the stimulation of his
sense of smell and the enjoyment of "arrangements" or movements ("swift,
deft, circular motions") that constitute a symbolic model of the "well-
ordered universe." Other senses are soon aroused. Platon addresses Pierre:

> "So you've seen a lot of troubles [*a mnogo vy nuzhdy uvidali*],
> eh, sir?" the little man suddenly said. And there was such a
> caressing and simple quality in that singsong voice of the man
> that Pierre wanted to reply, but his jaw trembled and tears came
> to his eyes. The little man gave Pierre no time to betray his
> confusion, but instantly continued in the same pleasant voice.
> "Eh, don't grieve, my dear," he said in the same gentle, caressing
> singsong voice in which old Russian peasant women talk. "Don't
> grieve, dear fellow: suffer an hour, live an age! That's how it
> is, my dear one. And here we live, God be praised, without
> offense. There are bad people to be found, but there are good
> ones, too," he said, and, while still speaking, he moved to his
> knees, then to his feet with an agile movement and, after clearing
> his throat, went off somewhere.

Pierre, whose interest in Platon till now has been confined to his sense
of smell and sight, now is touched by the *sound* of his voice: a tender,
motherly singsong voice that brings tears to his eyes. The mother-child
relationship now emerges clearly as Tolstoy's central metaphor in charac-
terizing Pierre's relationship to Platon. In the subsequent conversations
Tolstoy stresses Platon's motherly nature in general. Like a mother he
ministers to Pierre; he grieves over the fact that Pierre has no parents,
"especially no mother. A wife for counsel," he intones, "a mother-in-law
for a warm welcome, but there's none so dear as a man's own mother."
So, too, Platon grieves over "Moscow, mother of cities." "Round" and
nourishing like mother earth, Platon's first words to Pierre address them-

selves, significantly, to Pierre's "troubles" (*nuzhdy*—want, straits, need). And when he returns to him he brings, as one would expect of a mother, nourishment, food, in this case, potatoes. Pierre, who has not eaten for several days, finds the smell of the potatoes especially good. "Here, eat, sir . . . the potatoes are grand," says Platon, as he shows Pierre—almost as though he were a child—how to slice and eat the potato.

> It seemed to Pierre as though he had never eaten food more tasty than this. "Oh, I'm all right," Pierre said, "but why did they shoot these unfortunate people!*** The last one wasn't more than twenty." "Tsk, tsk***" said the little man. "It was a sin, a sin***" he added quickly and, as though his words were always ready in his mouth and unexpectedly flying out, he continued: "And how is it, sir, that you happened to remain in Moscow?" "I didn't think they would come so soon. I stayed on unexpectedly," Pierre said. "And how did they come to arrest you, my dear? in your house?" "No, I went to look at the fire, and there they seized me and tried me as an incendiary." "Where there's judgement there's injustice," interjected the little man. "And have you been here long?" asked Pierre as he munched the last potato.

Tolstoy's emphasis upon eating in this passage is no mere background detail. Pierre's return to normalcy is connected, finally, with food and the stimulation of his sense of *taste,* and even *touch* (the handling of the potato). Significantly, Tolstoy brackets the opening part of Pierre's conversation with Platon with the pleasures and ritual of eating. Pierre's very first words to Platon seem to signal as much the general satisfaction that comes from eating as a desire to minimize his concern for his own psychological or physical well-being. He is, of course, tormented by the killings. But the intensity of his anguish and moral concerns noticeably declines as he eats. Platon for his part hastily brushes aside Pierre's concern over the executions with a few words about sin. He turns the conversation immediately towards more concrete everyday questions: how did Pierre come to remain in Moscow? He is typically philosophical about Pierre's misfortune: all things balance out in life. It is indicative of the inner changes taking place in Pierre that he accepts Platon's Spinoza-like wisdom and forgets about his moral ache. The questions which torment Pierre—Tolstoy seems to suggest—cannot be answered on the plane of moral intellectual discourse; on a deeper, more organic level, however, these questions are "answered" by Pierre's munching of the last potato. His concern with "eternal" questions disappears with his potato; he addresses himself to issues of the moment: "And have you been here long?"

Tolstoy's juxtaposition of the insoluble questions of death and injustice with the pragmatic forces of life—here the instinctive need for, and enjoyment of, food—points to one of his most fundamental observations—that the vital life processes, the unconscious egoism of life, are totally indifferent to moral and intellectual "questions" of life and death or to the sense of the absurd in human existence. In the chapter on the execution of Devichii Field, for example, Tolstoy provides a chilling example of the way man's vital life processes remain numb even to the terrible reality of death: a prisoner, literally seconds before his execution, adjusts the tight knot on his blindfold; then he leans back against the bloody stake, but "feeling himself uncomfortable in this position he straightened himself, placed his feet evenly and leaned back more comfortably." In this extraordinary detail Tolstoy captures the terrible sense of the absurd and, at the same time, man's organic inability to face the reality of his own death. Pierre's munching of the potato at a moment of terrible moral anguish philosophically is of the same order as the prisoner's seemingly trivial but deeply instinctive concern for comfort a moment before total extinction. Here the "blindfold"—one may note in passing—as an image speaks eloquently not only of man's quite conscious unwillingness to "look death in the face," but of the quite *natural* and *unconscious* blindfold afforded by the egoism of life. A capacity guilelessly to embed, as it were, an everyday image in a deep substratum of anthropological or philosophical thought is characteristic, of course, of Tolstoy's unsurpassed art.

Tolstoy's attitude toward the egoism of life was deeply ambivalent. The indifference of nature-in-man to the insoluble questions that stir him disturbed Tolstoy because he recognized its tendency to displace the ethical vision. At the same time, he recognized the action of this egoism of life as necessary to the continuation of life and as tonic and restorative in the human organism. In such later works as *The Death of Ivan Ilych* Tolstoy, of course, concentrates savagely and with enormous satiric power upon the banality and moral-spiritual emptiness of the egoism of life. This satiric sense is quite alive in an early work, "The Three Deaths," where Tolstoy, for example, juxtaposes the husband's enjoyment of his food with his apparent grief over his dying wife. But in general in this story Tolstoy evaluates the egoism of life in a positive way: a healthy orientation toward death in a healthy individual or society, he believes, should not (and does not—where peasants are concerned) exclude open recognition of the life forces. Life and death, then, should confront each other freely, without restraint or dissembling, as they do in nature.

Tolstoy's approach in *War and Peace* towards the egoism of life is philosophically close to his position in "The Three Deaths." But while he affirms in his great epic that man can attain some inner harmony and happiness only by allowing himself in some measure to be ruled by the organic inner drives and processes of life and nature, he does not cease to honor the pressure in man to address the great moral, social and philosophical questions of life and death, justice and injustice, right and wrong; he cannot, and does not wish to, disengage himself from the vital questions of the meaning of life. The rhythmic, almost patterned swings and alternations in the spiritual dramas of Pierre Bezukhov and Prince Andrei attest to Tolstoy's own permanent moral and spiritual restlessness. The equilibrium of a Platon Karataev, on the other hand, is maintained only by disregarding or evading the painful social and ethical questions of life, by adopting a fatalistic outlook—one that gives expression, indeed, to the objective conditions of his life. Pierre notes in the first epilogue to *War and Peace* that Platon most likely would not have approved of his new political and social activities, but that he definitely would have approved of his "family life"; he "desired so much to find seemliness, happiness and tranquility in everything." Platon, quite clearly, gives his full blessing to the nesting principle.

In the final lines of the chapter depicting Pierre's encounter with Platon, Tolstoy writes: "Sounds of crying and shouting were heard somewhere outside and in the distance, and fires could be seen through the cracks in the shed; but in the shed it was quiet and dark. Pierre did not sleep for a long time, but lay in the darkness with open eyes listening to the measured snoring of Platon who was lying next to him, and he felt that the formerly wrecked universe now was beginning to move in his soul, but with a new beauty and on new, unshakeable foundations."

This final scene in the darkness of Platon's shed is rich in content. The transcendental vision, or sense of inner transfiguration, comes to Pierre, significantly, as he lies childlike and secure beside the motherly Platon. His rhythmic snoring, like the lapping of waters against Prince Andrei's ferry, symbolizes the ever sustaining life rhythms of nature. This is a moment of second birth for Pierre, an awakening to a "new beauty," a new sense of coherence and organicity in life. The cycle of Pierre's regeneration is complete. In a symbolic sense, Pierre had "died" on Devichii Field. Yet his trauma was both destructive and constructive: it destroyed his "universe," but at the same time created the conditions for a new synthesis of psychic being. Pierre's encounter with Platon is momentous; it constitutes in the largest sense the apogee of his inner quest for identity with the people, the collective, the organic forces of Russian life—a quest that crystallizes in his wandering at Borodino. In psychic terms his meeting with Platon takes on the character of a "return to the mother," to a primordial situation or "first state" whence new creation becomes possible. Pierre's symbolic return to the womb thus takes on the paradoxical form of a renewal of life. Pierre had rightly sensed after Devichii Field that the possibility for renewal did not lie within his power. Platon emerges here as the source and symbol of renewal: as earth-mother, mother Russia, the people—the indestructible reality of the matrix. Pierre's "resurrection" is accompanied, appropriately, by a sense of rebirth of the world, an experience of movement of the universe.

This final moment in the shed, however, is not without a certain ambiguity, the kind that is characteristic of all "resolutions" or denouements in *War and Peace,* including its great epilogue (1). Tolstoy does not conceal the negative component that inheres in the "return to the mother"; he does not hide an unpleasant truth—one that is symbolized by the same rhythmic snoring of Platon—that such interior harmony as we obtain in this world involves in some measure an exclusion of the fiery world of wails and shouts, that is, all that can be seen and heard even through the cracks in Platon's shed.

"How can he who has magnificence of mind and is the spectator of all time and existence," asks Plato in *The Republic,* "think much of human life?" Tolstoy could only have responded ambivalently to these words: for it was his destiny as man and artist to experience "all time and all existence," yet at the same time to "think much of human life." Indeed, it was precisely in his moments of experience of all time and existence that he raised the sharpest questions about the meaning of life—a meaning which for him, in spite of his own perfect realization of life, was deeply moral and social. "Not for me is the only possible happiness," exclaims Olenin in *The Cossacks* as he looks back on his lost dream of an organic life close to nature.

Tolstoy—unlike Plato—in the final analysis remains within the circle of the Protagorean concept of "man as the measure of all things." The fiery light and the shouts and wails outside Platon's shed constitute an ineluctable human reality in Tolstoy's world; they bespeak disharmony and conflict rather than Platonic harmonies; they agitate the spirit and befog the mind. If we allow for a genuine allusion to Plato's "cave" in the scene in Karataev's shed, then we must recognize an embryonic element that threatens the Platonic idyll. Plato uses the cave and its inhabitants to illustrate man's false sense of the reality of human existence (the shadows flickering on the wall before the eyes of the underground prisoners); he uses it to demonstrate the actuality of the ideal reality which lies outside the perception of ordinary men. Pierre absorbs a sense of this ideal reality from his mentor Platon in the shed. Yet the beauty, harmony and coherence that are the transcendental Platonic vision, Tolstoy seems to suggest, may in fact in the moral universe of man turn out to be *false images* that beautify the fiery world of suffering, pain and death. In the most extreme case, knowledge of this world can destroy one's "faith in a well-ordered universe." Such, indeed, is the "cold white light" of Prince Andrei's perception of death before the battle of Borodino, a light which destroys "the false images which had agitated, enthralled and tormented [him] . . . the principal pictures of the magic lantern of life." Such is the knowledge which momentarily shatters Pierre's well-ordered universe on Devichii Field. But in the dark and quiet of Platon's shed, lying next to him, Pierre's spiritual energies are renewed. He is prepared to go forth into the world again, to undertake a journey which will lead him—if we read the first epilogue to *War and Peace* attentively—once again into the fiery light and shouts and wails of human existence.

Platon Karataev, Tolstoy suggests, is for Pierre a "precious memory," an idea, almost a figment of the imagination. He forever remained for Pierre, Tolstoy writes in the chapter following the encounter in the shed, "what he had seemed that first night: an unfathomable, round and eternal personification of the spirit of simplicity and truth." Pierre's first awareness of Platon was through a "strong smell of sweat." In time, it would seem, that smell passed into memory where memory transfigured it. Platon's "words and actions," Tolstoy writes in the concluding lines of the chapter where he speaks of the nature of Pierre's recollections of Platon, "flowed from him as evenly, inevitably and spontaneously as fragrance [*zapakh*] emanates from a flower." Thus, the second birth of Pierre Bezukhov is simultaneously the creation of a Russian icon—Platon Karataev.

A Man Speaking to Men: The Narratives of *War and Peace*

W. Gareth Jones

Entranced by a night spent outside a military camp in the Caucasus in 1851, the twenty-three-year-old Tolstoy wrote in his diary, "I thought—I'll go and describe what I see. But how to write it? One needs to go and sit down at an ink-stained desk, take some grey paper and ink; get one's fingers dirty and trace letters on the paper. The letters make up words, the words— sentences; but is it possible to convey the feeling? Is it not possible some- how to pour into another man one's view at the sight of nature?" The young soldier was discomfited by the artificiality of writing, by an aware- ness of the fallibility of words. But in this jotting he had already signalled that the aim of writing for him went beyond composing something of intrinsic worth, poetry so well wrought that it could pretend to an inde- pendent existence. Parable would later be exalted by Tolstoy over poetry; not merely because the former carried a moral message, but because the parable was an art of performance, "pouring one's view into another man," demanding an attentive and responsive listener. Writing for him, as for Wordsworth, meant "a man speaking to men," and Tolstoy would occa- sionally enhance this sense of public performance by equating writing with singing to his fellow men. In the sketches for his *Childhood,* for example, it was to music that he turned for an analogy to explain his new kind of writing that would avoid stale convention in its direct "anti-poetic" appeal to his reader. Significantly, it was not the musician as creative composer that suggested himself to Tolstoy but the *performing* artist; the image that

From *New Essays on Tolstoy,* edited by Malcolm V. Jones. © 1978 by Cambridge University Press.

he held of himself was not that of the song writer, but of the singer, intent on affecting his audience.

What is remarkable about Tolstoy is that he never saw himself as a solitary singer set apart from a world of passive listeners. His world's stage was peopled by men and women with their own voices, speaking and singing parts they had fashioned for themselves, listening as responsively as an audience for parables. So were his novels. For it was this Tolstoyan understanding that inspired his works: human society consisted of men, each pouring his feelings into another. His creatures live on the page because they too, like him, make sense of existence by narrating their experiences to each other. One must see *War and Peace* not as a single narrative issuing from one author, but as a dynamic pattern of many narratives, constantly varied and interreacting. To be Tolstoy's reader, so far as this novel is concerned, one's response must be not to the author's tale, but to the work's many narratives.

For Tolstoy was accustomed to imagine his fictional characters, like himself, as performers; often his creatures, in contrast to those of other novelists, do not engage in private conversation, cogitation or reflection but hold forth publicly, narrating, recounting or "telling stories"—*rasska-zyvat'* is the Russian verb for which it is difficult to find a single English equivalent. They speak to a company who respond as a distanced audience to a ritualised performance. So at the beginning of *War and Peace,* Prince Vasily talks "like an actor speaking lines from an old play," Anna Scherer enthuses "in order not to disappoint people's expectations," the vicomte de Mortemart is introduced as "un parfait conteur." Much time and mental energy was spent by Tolstoy in the search for a beginning that would set his *War and Peace* in motion; over a dozen false starts are recorded. What is significant about the final choice—the description of a soirée at which the main protagonists are guests was hardly a fresh solution—is the way in which modes of narration, or communication between people, are presented and examined. It is as if Tolstoy, on the threshold of his own storytelling, wished to put his reader on his guard against its conventions and artifice by demonstrating to him different kinds of narration. First there is the polish and assurance of the vicomte de Mortemart's refined reciting of a scabrous anecdote about Napoleon and the duc d'Enghien, a piece of society gossip greeted with delight by his audience. Set against that, the earnest conversation of Pierre and the abbé Morio on the balance of power is shown, for all its sincerity, to be out of place and awkward. In Anna Scherer's salon, the *well told* anecdote, however superficial, always wins more attention than any attempt to bumble out the truth. Even a nonsensical buffoon's tale from Prince Hippolyte gains more respect than Pierre's honest theorising.

What is happening in these early scenes, as the reader commits himself to the long journey through Tolstoy's novel, is that the author is signalling to him some of the curious relationships between the man who tells the story and his listener. An attempt to tell the honest truth unconventionally, as by Pierre, is met with resistance; there may be more real communing, not only in the retailing of superficial gossip related with polished art, but even in twaddle such as Hippolyte's nonsense tale which makes everyone stop to listen and applaud.

Without making any separate declaration on the nature of his art, Tolstoy had embedded within his own narrative the awareness that had come to him under the Caucasian night sky: experience cannot be conveyed directly to another; the paraphernalia of art is necessary for any human communication. The same realisation had been fused into the narrative of *The Raid* (1853), where Captain Khlopov, so rich in life's experiences, can only seek to convey those experiences to a young volunteer by suggesting that he read the historian Mikhaylovsky-Danilevsky and chat to a young poet in the regiment (chap. 1). Aware that experienced truth was invariably modified by the artifices needed for its transmission, Tolstoy felt impelled to alert his reader to the extent to which he was being manipulated by fiction's conventions. So, as *War and Peace* was set in motion, its reader was warned to distrust its apparent solidity and fascination.

This insinuation into his fiction of passages that encouraged the reader to determine consciously his own attitude to narrative (whether to listen avidly along with most of Anna Scherer's guests, or turn away in disgust as Prince Andrey did from the anecdote about Napoleon) was not new for Tolstoy. If the examination of the relationship between narrator and audience is there at the beginning of *War and Peace* as it was in *The Raid*, it lay too at the foundation of Tolstoy's first published work, *Childhood*. In the sketches for that work, it is apparent how much more important enthralling and moving his reader was for Tolstoy than weaving verbal patterns. By the final version, a perusal of the bond between author and audience had been incorporated into the fiction in the central chapter "Verses" where the boy, Nikolenka, faced with the task of producing a present for his grandmother's name day, recites a poem for her. It is not as an entertainer that Nikolenka is presented but as an embryonic Tolstoyan narrator, beset with disgust and self-doubt, and fearful of his reception. In

the boy's composing, Tolstoy revealed to his reader the inspiration, dogged-
ness, plagiarism and posing involved in producing an inherently false communication to the listener of an initially sincere impulse.

There are times in *War and Peace* when Tolstoy becomes almost Brecht-
ian in the relentless warning to his readers against being swept along by
his narrative, particularly of the historical and military events. Again, however, no separate artistic manifesto is apparent; rather we are allowed, as
in *Childhood*, to see the relationship between narrator and audience developing between the fictive characters. Inevitably, in such a work as *War and
Peace*, with character and episodes embedded in a historical chronicle, the
registering of event, time, place, conversation bears the novel along. Is
Nikolay Rostov's arrival in Tilsit significant because he arrived there on
June 27, 1807? Tolstoy's noting of that day is reminiscent of the conventional
chronicler: "That day, 27 June, the first conditions of peace were signed.
The Emperors exchanged orders: Alexander received the Légion d'Hon-
neur, and Napoleon the St Andrew 1st Class, and that day a dinner was
arranged for the Preobrazhensky regiment given to it by a battalion of the
French Guards." Yet this sort of brisk narrative of Tolstoy's, making immediate the public, historical framework for private happenings, had just
been put in question in the previous chapter where Boris Drubetskoy's
habit of noting down particulars, even at the Tilsit meeting between the
Emperors, had been mocked. It is Boris here who stands for the typical
writer who stores up material with which he will later seek to affect an
audience. Not only does he make a note of the persons present and their
uniforms, but is meticulous about logging time: "At the very moment
when the emperors entered the pavilion, he looked at his watch and did
not forget to look again at the moment when Alexander left the pavilion.
The meeting had lasted 1 hour 53 minutes: that is what he noted that evening
among other facts which he supposed had historical significance." This
ironic comment on memoir writing that concentrates on surface detail while
telling nothing about the true condition of human relationship is again made
through a narrating character, one of the "performers" in the fiction, and
not by Tolstoy himself. Ironically, it gives the reader an eloquent warning
against narrative chronology used with effect by the author of *War and
Peace*.

If Tolstoy wished to warn his reader against the conventional chronicling of diplomatic history, he was even more intent on setting him on
guard against the narration of military exploits. And on guard against the
reader's own craving for the conventional. It is through Nikolay Rostov—

as much, surely, an emanation of Tolstoy's self as Prince Andrey and Pierre—and his recital of Schöngraben, that Tolstoy persuades his own reader to understand that however truthful a narrator would wish to be, he is swayed from the truth by his audience that is bound to rely on conventional signals. Transparent truth cannot be seen. Art's untruth springs not necessarily from the maliciousness of an embellishing narrator, but is demanded by an audience that relies on the conventional. So does Nikolay's audience: "They expected an account of how he was all on fire, beside himself, how he rushed like a storm at the square; how he was hacked at, while striking to left and right; how a sabre cut into his flesh and he fell into oblivion, and so on. And he recounted all that for them." It is interesting that Tolstoy had once shared Rostov's feelings. In his note to the fourth volume of the Tolstoy Centenary Edition *Tales of Army Life,* Aylmer Maude recalled that "One day, when talking about Sevastopol, he [Tolstoy] told me that when writing these sketches he was aware that, contending with his desire to tell the truth as he saw it, there was another feeling prompting him to say what was expected of him." The point is made clearly to the reader of *War and Peace* that there are conventional ways of recounting battles that are inherently false; paradoxically it is only these false strokes that can shape an experience for an audience. Tolstoy does not propose to spurn these conventions, but would like his reader to be aware of them, and see *through* them to the real experience.

The lesson is well placed: the probing of Nikolay's "imperceptible, involuntary and inevitable" slide into untruth must modify the reader's acceptance of the description of Andrey's wounding which follows shortly. At Austerlitz, from the moment that Prince Andrey shouts "Hurrah!" and raises the standard to rally his men, the charge is recounted in a conventional manner. It is with the panache of jingoistic literature that the scene is told initially: the banner is held aloft, bullets whistle, men fall to left and right of our hero—it is as if we are listening again to Nikolay entertaining his audience. Already prepared by the insight into the gap between the conventional style of Nikolay's story of Schöngraben and the true experience which it obscured, the reader, following Andrey's charge, is swept along by the vigorous conventional description, but simultaneously suspects the truthfulness of the account. He may remember that it was the same Prince Andrey who had stemmed Nikolay's increasingly impassioned narrative, borne beyond convention into cliché, silencing him with his unexpected appearance. The reader is, therefore, prepared for the sudden dissolution of the conventional here as the same Andrey asks "What are they doing?"

on seeing the wordless but mortal tug-of-war between a French and Russian soldier. From that point on, we are subject to a new narrative technique—but not at the expense of old conventions.

If the experience of warfare, as indeed all human experience, was beyond man's ability to comprehend and narrate, why should Tolstoy have persisted so long with his writing? Tolstoy mediates his answer through a Nikolay Rostov made fully conscious of the perils of communication between men. After his experience of Austerlitz and the 1807 campaigns, Nikolay had realised that "in recounting military events, men always lie, as he himself had lied while recounting." So it is with shame that he listens to an overblown account of a patriotic exploit by General Rayevsky while providing his own debunking gloss to the narration in his mind. Yet he does not object to the narration. And the reason that Nikolay gives to himself might well be Tolstoy's apologia for continuing to write fiction, despite his rage for the truth. Such narration, he came to realise, even if it failed to communicate experience fully, had a particular justification; despite its falsity it exerted an independent moral force and enabled men to commune with each other in society. For Tolstoy this was no new revelation. The earlier Nikolenka of *Childhood* had also realised, as a consumer of literature, the way in which the lie of art enhanced the art of living. The vividness of the children's games was sharpened by their imitation of *Swiss Family Robinson*. Although Nikolenka knew as well as his supercilious elder brother Volodya that a stick was not a gun, his play was all the more intense if he pretended. The rhetorical question posed by the child to close the chapter "Games" in *Childhood,* might still be the one for Nikolay Rostov to ponder over: "If one is to judge by reality, then there would be no play. And without play, what would remain?"

II

If the Nikolenka of *Childhood* was unsettled—and the reader in consequence—by his growing awareness of the fictive fluidity of verses, and story-based games, he was no more secure in the language, or it would be more correct to say languages, that shaped the expression of his experiences. *War and Peace,* which has been called a bilingual novel for its large use of French, was by no means the first work in which Tolstoy had troubled the reader with a foreign language. If *War and Peace* begins in French, then the first spoken dialogue in *Childhood* is in German between Karl Ivanich, the family tutor, and Nikolenka. While the use of German may be explained as historical colouring, as the work progresses we become aware that Tolstoy intended to present his child as one conscious of the lack of security afforded by human speech. Although the mother speaks Russian with the children, her own mother tongue, and the one she employs for her intimate thoughts, is German. The shift of language is noticed by the child as he perceives that French is used at the dinner table formally to exclude Grigory, the holy fool, from the community around the table. Foreign idiom was a means for Tolstoy to intimate to his reader his sense of the fragility of language as a means of communication.

The use of French, and to a lesser extent German, in *War and Peace* as well, is a means by which the reader is made aware of the linguistic texture of the fictional work. Too aware, perhaps, for many early reviewers—not only the young radical nationalist critics, but also Tolstoy's aristocratic friends—protested against an apparent overindulgence in French. Indeed the novel begins with a sentence whose single Russian word is used as a calculated disparagement, "Eh bien, mon prince, Gênes et Lucques ne sont plus que des apanages, des *pomest'ya,* de la famille Buonaparte." Since it is Anna Scherer who speaks these words, it would seem natural for her to speak French and so it seemed to the editors of the Jubilee Edition who maintained that *War and Peace* would make no sense without French since French was an "integral accessory to the way of life of the upper class at the beginning of the nineteenth century." Had they chosen to follow the 1873 edition in which the French had been translated, they argued, many of the characters, such as Anna Scherer, Hippolyte Kuragin, Bilibin, Napoleon, Kutuzov, Alexander I, would lose some of their individual quality. It was roughly these reasons—historical and dramatic—that Tolstoy himself gave as a rational justification for his apparently excessive use of French. Prompted by subsequent criticism from friends, however, Tolstoy allowed the 1873 edition to appear not only with the removal of his philosophical and historical discursions, but with all the French translated. This he did, however, with some regret. The use of French, despite what Tolstoy's editors and Tolstoy as editor of his own work suggested, goes far beyond the need for local colouring. Could he not have merely indicated the use of French, as contemporary critics suggested? There are times when Tolstoy does indeed state that his characters whose dialogue is given in Russian, are conversing in French; this is true even in the case of Andrey and Natasha. Furthermore the abundant gallicisms of the novel might have been sufficient to preserve the local historical colouring. However, French is not merely used for historical *vraisemblance.* Sometimes it would appear that French is used to stress artificiality of sentiment and attitude, as opposed to the genuineness of Russian: it is the language in which Pierre proposes to Hélène, the language in which Hélène addresses Natasha at the opera. For Andrey, it is not only Natasha's gaiety and shyness that are a mark of her naturalness, but her mistakes in French. However, some characters manage to be intensely Russian despite their French, such as Kutuzov with his fondness for Madame de Genlis's novels and French proverbs, or Bilibin who showed an "exceptionally Russian fearlessness before self-judgement and self-mockery" in a long letter to Prince Andrey despite his writing it "in French with French jokes and turns of phrase." Bilibin is one of the most conscious of Tolstoy's narrating characters, producing memorable phrases in his "inner laboratory" that insignificant people could carry from drawing room to drawing room. And one of the features that ensures that the reader grasps the mechanical precision of Bilibin's narrations is his skill at mixing French and Russian, "saying in Russian only those words which he wished to emphasise disparagingly."

It is this mingling of French with Russian which is met in the novel's first sentence, rather than the use of French itself that makes the reader linguistically unsettled, as were the early critics who would have felt more comfortable in the presence of *War and Peace* had Tolstoy spiked his Russian with less French. It was an experience that the English reader of Jane Austen, or even Dickens with his idiosyncratic idiom, never endured: English, the common mother tongue of writer and reader, ensured some stability in their relationship. Even this bedrock of communication was deliberately undermined by Tolstoy. The insidious French in his narrative is subversive, alerting the reader to the transience of language and the words used by the writer to communicate with him. In excusing his use of French, in *A Few Words about "War and Peace,"* Tolstoy drew an analogy with the formal texture of a painting. The French, he explained, was akin to the dark patches used by a painter; they may be perceived as shadows, but the naive eye sees them as black blobs. "I would only wish that those who find it amusing that Napoleon speaks Russian and French in turn, would realise that they find it so only because they, like a man looking at a portrait, see not a face with light and shade, but a black patch under a nose." However, what is striking about the analogy is how Tolstoy reveals his awareness that his use of French actually encouraged his reader to see through the conventional deceptive shadows of the artist to the dark, crude blobs of paint at the base of his craft. Language, too, may be as inexpressive as a paint pot.

Differing languages disturb the reader; he shares the experience of Prince Andrey, conscious of confusion on the battlefield when he hears the Babel of a multi-lingual exchange. "Pfuel . . . shouted angrily even at Wolzogen "Nun ja, was soll denn da noch expliziert werden?"—Paulucci and Michaud in a duet attacked Wolzogen in French. Armfelt addressed Pfuel in German. Tol explained it in Russian to Prince Bolkonsky. Prince Andrey listened in silence, and observed."

III

It is that coolly observant listener, like Andrey, that Tolstoy would have liked his reader to be. Our discussion to this point has attempted to bring out the way in which, through his "narrating" characters, Tolstoy has warned his reader against the deceit of storytelling. In wishing to make the reader aware in this way of the ritual of narration, Tolstoy seeks to elicit a special response from him, engaging him in the particular conspiracy in which the true novelist would wish to embroil his reader.

Readers of *War and Peace,* will, of course, object that they are surely not always treated by Tolstoy as cool, aristocratic observers of the world's stage. Sometimes there is a direct appeal to us as one of a mutinous mob. The coarse demagogic address is particularly apparent in Tolstoy's excursions into historiography. By showing the absurdity of other versions of historical events, he suggests that it must follow that "ours"—that is, the author and reader in collusion—our version must be true. Dealing with the battle of Borodino, Tolstoy gave his own precis of the view of "all historians" and then declared with the most conventional of debating ploys: "That is what the histories say, and all that is completely unjust, which can easily be vouched for by anybody who wishes to look into the essentials of the matter." In then giving a revised account of Borodino, Tolstoy flatters the reader; we feel that we are privileged to know more about the battle than any learned historian. Again at the beginning of part 3 we have the same tub-thumper's appeal to his audience: historians are wrong is the message, the implication being—and it is never more than an implication— that Tolstoy is right. And the debater's claim is supported by crude, simplistic mechanistic images: any fool can realise that it is not the hands of a clock that cause church bells to ring, nor is it its whistle that sets a locomotive running.

Yet even when his demagoguery is at its most effective, we find Tolstoy recoiling from it and subjecting it to the same criticism as other forms of conventional communication. One of the most effective of the scenes debunking historiography is that in which Lavrushka, Nikolay Rostov's servant, falls into the hands of the French. This interlude was based on a passage from Thiers's history which recounted the capture of a Russian whom the French took to be a Cossack, "un enfant du Don," who showed a childlike wonder at being in the presence of the great Napoleon; the Emperor responded by freeing the Cossack and sending him back to the Russian lines, an action which is described by Thiers in an overblown, romantic and, consequently for Tolstoy, false phrase to which the reader's attention is drawn: "Napoléon . . . lui fit donner la liberté, comme à un oiseau qu'on rend aux champs qui l'ont vu naître." In reality Tolstoy would have us believe, it was not a noble savage of a Cossack that the French had captured, but Nikolay's wily lackey who, far from being impressed by Napoleon, realised that his role was to pretend astonishment and veneration. If the scene had ended there, then it would have been unconvincing, another example of Tolstoy's crude haranguing. Even if we are led to distrust Thiers's narrative, common sense suggests to us as we read the passage that there was little likelihood of Thiers's historical "Cossack" being the fictional Lavrushka.

But the scene did not end with the freeing of Lavrushka. And as Lavrushka returns to the Russian lines, Tolstoy submits his own previous narrative to a critical appraisal through the mind of his character. Even more striking than Lavrushka's hoodwinking of Napoleon are his thoughts as he rides back: "he galloped towards the forward posts, thinking up beforehand everything that had not been and that he would recount to his own side. Everything which had really happened to him, he did not wish to recount just because that seemed to him unworthy of a narrative."

As Lavrushka returns to his lines, the point is forcibly made—strikingly soon after Tolstoy's attempt to "tell the truth" by debunking Thiers and his "enfant du Don"—that the substance of man's life is incommunicable. Lavrushka knows, as his master Nikolay did, that conventions which channel the flow of communication from narrator to listener will inevitably frustrate any stories he cares to tell based on perceived events. What he "thinks up," or what comes to his mind, as he gallops back is a story to tell, not wholly unrelated to his experience, but "worthy of being recounted." Lavrushka and Nikolay like Nikolenka of *Childhood* and Captain Khlopov of *The Raid* before them are aware that what is recognised as "worthy of recounting" is the only possible way for one person to communicate through speech with his fellows. Lavrushka is here, like his master previously, involuntarily and inevitably moved into untruth, despite his desire to tell things as they had happened.

For Tolstoy perhaps, Lavrushka could have only given voice to the truth through instinctive song—if he had been indeed Thiers's "bird restored to its native fields." Tolstoy had anticipated many writers who would feel how words are so much more haphazard and fugitive as a medium of expression compared with song. In the drafts for *Childhood* where he had sought an analogy for writing in music two types of singers were described—the "head singer," bound by technique, and the "chest singer," who sang more directly to his audience. The latter, the instinctive performer rather than the trained musician, reappears a number of times in *War and Peace.* So Natasha at the end of the second volume's first part is the typical, intuitively physical, "chest singer":

> Natasha took her first note, her throat widened, her chest straightened, her eyes took on a serious expression. She did not think of anyone or anything at that moment, and from the lips, set in a smile, poured sounds, those sounds which anyone can produce at the same periods of time, the same intervals but which leave you a thousand times unmoved, and at the thousand and first make you shudder and weep.

Again it is not the beauty of Natasha's art that Tolstoy wished his reader to appreciate, since Natasha with her "untrained voice, with her incorrect breathing and strained phrasing" is as "antipoetic" as Tolstoy wished to be. But techniques can never be a substitute for sincere human expression such as the singing voice. "Her voice had that virginal inviolability, that unawareness of its strength and that unpolished velvet quality which so merged with the mistakes in the art of singing that it seemed impossible to change anything in that voice without spoiling it." There is an assurance in Natasha's singing, stressed by the set of her stride—a firm heel to toe movement—as she takes up her position. This same stride is repeated when she finds so much delight in the sound of her own voice as she goes through her singing exercises while waiting for Andrey: the rhythm of the voice exercises here gives way to the more elemental rhythm, in which she finds equal pleasure, of her heel and toe striking the parquet, "just as joyfully as to the sounds of her voice, she listened intently to the measured tap of her heel and the squeak of the toe." Tolstoy was clearly fascinated by the primitive naive instinctive art of singing which somehow was not aimed at communication, was not therefore circumscribed by technique, yet somehow communicated directly with listeners—the type of folk singing practised by the Rostovs' uncle: "Uncle sang as the peasant folk sing, in the full and naive conviction that in song all the meaning is in the words alone, that the tune comes of itself and that there is never a separate tune and that the tune is only there to hold it together." So the tune was unconscious, "Like the tune of a bird." The idea of song bursting forth from man's lips as from a bird's throat, as an unconscious affirmation of self, is again suggested in the description of Platon Karatayev's singing: "He sang songs not like singers knowing that they are heard but sang, as birds sing, evidently because it was as necessary to emit these sounds, as it is necessary to join in song or break off." For Karatayev, and the uncle, for the people, singing is a means of self-affirmation and there need be no thought of the audience. It is not a prerogative of the common folk, however. It is the same unconscious delight that Natasha experiences in her voice exercises in the resonant drawingroom. For her, a failure to sing becomes a signal of her collapse after the break with Andrey; her restoration to health is marked by the renewal of the ability to sing. What Tolstoy shows in these singing passages is the necessity for human voicing of a reality which may be expressible but not wholly communicable. The listeners—one might even say the eavesdroppers on these naive, bird-like effusions—can only be stirred by the contagion with a deeper reality so distant from the surface manifestations of existence, such as those noted and registered by Boris Drubetskoy. Song is heard at climactic moments in *War and Peace,* and it would appear that Tolstoy was as taken by the idea of pure expression being possible through music as was Paul Valéry in his conviction that music was the ideal art.

Tolstoy's medium, however, was words, even if words did not spring so freshly from men's lips as song. Sometimes they may: they fell naturally from Platon Karatayev's lips so that he could not understand words taken in isolation, nor could he repeat what had been said. Language could, as in his case, flow along as an integral component of the life of the moment. Just as Natasha, unable to explain her experiences *in words* to Andrey when their love was at its most intense, made Andrey understand her despite the lack of articulation. As in love, so in war: Kutuzov at the height of battle does not rely on words alone but on the expression of the narrator and his tone. So the reader, following the words on the page, paradoxically is alerted to the dimness of words at climactic moments in man's life.

Thus, while using the full power of his rhetoric to sustain his fiction, Tolstoy intimates to his reader through Karatayev, Kutuzov and Bilibin, through the mingling of French with Russian, the insignificance and deception of words. In writing history with irony and persuasion, he alerts his reader, through Boris Drubetskoy, to distrust all historical narration. In reading Tolstoy's magnificent set pieces of adventure, heroism and love, the reader is reminded of Nikolay Rostov's and Lavrushka's realisation that it is only possible to mediate a modicum of true experience through narration. In the end, the reader puts his trust in Tolstoy, since he is being fashioned by an author who endeavours to let him take a critical stance. If

Tolstoy as an omniscient narrator plays God with his creation, then he sets out not to predetermine his reader's responses but to endow him with critical free will.

IV

The passages where Tolstoy seems to reach out to his reader to alert and instruct him are remarkable for not being set apart from the main narrative. The problem of communication for Tolstoy was never reduced to a question of mere technique but was fully integrated into a particular Tolstoyan vision. So, although Tolstoy may use the chapter "Verses" in *Childhood* to mediate his views on literary composition and its reception, that chapter is simultaneously a central scene in the work, placed at the point where a farewell has been sung to childhood as the boy became conscious of self in relation to others. Time after time, the reader finds that the characters' narrative performances within Tolstoy's main narrative are fused with emotional points of crisis in the novel. It is indeed a feature of Tolstoy's fictional universe to find characters at a high emotional pitch reading or writing, being in an audience or telling a story. At life's turning points, the art of narration intrudes. Two examples from the second volume of the second part will suffice: Pierre, on his way to Petersburg after his duel and break with his wife, is beset with nihilistic thoughts which are reinforced by his reading of an epistolary novel by Madame Suza (a writer despised by Tolstoy) which prompts him to compare his own situation and that of Hélène with the story of "some Amélie de Mansfeld." By the time Pierre arrives in Petersburg, after his conversion to freemasonry, he spends whole days reading Thomas à Kempis. From Madame Suza to Thomas à Kempis! Their narratives are shown to have influenced Pierre's life, revealed his instability and moved him from nihilistic despair to certitude. When shortly, in chapter 10, we cut to Prince Andrey at Bald Hills, *War and Peace* appears briefly to become an epistolary novel as Andrey opens two letters, one from his father and the other from Bilibin. Off stage, Andrey's son is hovering between life and death in the nursery. Yet Bilibin's letter, written in French, bristling with sardonic irony, consciously a literary creation aiming for effect, manages to capture Andrey's whole attention so that it is only with an effort of will that he can shake off his bondage to Bilibin's artificial narrating, and return to the solid reality of the nursery. Throughout the ensuing scene, the reader is conscious that this father, despite his deep feelings for his son, has been infected and somehow modified by his recent reading, so that he preserves—even in the private solitude of the nursery—

some of Bilibin's diplomatic restraint: "Prince Andrey wanted to seize, squeeze, press to his breast this small helpless being; he did not dare do it."

What we should recognise is that the narrative mode itself is often employed to precipitate feelings. In both the above cases we have stock figures from fiction: the despairing cuckold of a cold wife, the distressed father of a dying son. The reader would expect the conventional novelist to limit himself to a description or dramatisation of that despair, of that distress. Tolstoy, however, does not attempt to describe these states directly; the ultimate reality of distress, pain or joy is indescribable. They are too complex. Mingled with Pierre's despair unto death is an irritating enjoyment of his emotional state; with Andrey's brimming paternal love, there is an admixture of cold aloofness and male exasperation at being shackled to domesticity. These complexes of emotion may be vented in such acts as intuitive song, or mutely in a brisk walk, such as Natasha's heeling and toeing in her drawing room. But if they are to be cast into words, then such states are best given shape through the medium of some formal address or narration which may well be tangential to the real experience. So the nature of Pierre's *pleasurable* despair is made evident in his reading of Madame Suza. It is Bilibin's letter, exquisite in its artificiality, that brings out the full complexity of Andrey's genuine emotional state.

The second volume from which the above examples are taken is a section of *War and Peace* where the love affairs of the novel are developed, if not resolved: Pierre is reunited with Hélène, Prince Andrey asks for Natasha's hand in marriage, Nikolay declares his love for Sonya, Boris Drubetskoy and Julie Karagina make their match, and Natasha is seduced by Anatole. It appears that Tolstoy had set out to examine the thousand faces of love in tracing these matches and mismatches. Again a framework of novelistic convention can be seen around each affair: faithful love being put to the test of absence, love triumphing over impediments of social station, a marriage of convenience, a conventional seduction. However, once more Tolstoy shows how rapport is made not in discussion or even conversation, but emerges through men's use of those many forms of narrative that have been elaborated in human culture. Before following these manifestations of love it is worth noting at the outset that the reader is reminded of the futility of trying to transfer one's vision directly to another. During Pierre's address to his brother freemasons on a way of regenerating the world, the reader is told that Pierre was driven by the need "to convey his thought of another exactly as he understood it." That, for Tolstoy, is the impossibility. The lodge reacts as negatively to Pierre's honesty as Anna Scherer's salon had: not only those opposed to his views reject him, but even those in general agreement misunderstand him. The result of this confusion is that Pierre is awkwardly reunited with his wife. The awkwardness of that dutiful cohabitation is, of course, an unstable foundation for the love affairs that follow. If the cohabitation had been made possible by a rational address, then it is other forms of narrative—song, mumming, sentimental literature, music, opera and dramatic readings—that determine the relationships that ensue. Their common feature is that they are all addressed to an audience. They are all performances.

Without being informed by the narrator, the reader realises that Prince Andrey comes to full realisation of his love for Natasha when she sings at the clavichord. His falling in love is fixed in time and place as if it were a religious conversion. One is reminded of Paul Claudel's memory of his own conversion, so rooted in the Christmas of 1886 in Notre Dame "on the right, opposite the vestry by the second pillar before the choir" as he responded to the singing.

> Prince Andrey stood at the window, conversing with the ladies and listening to her. In the middle of a phrase Prince Andrey fell silent and had a sudden feeling that his throat was filling with tears whose possibility he had not known in himself. He looked at the singing Natasha, and something new and joyful happened in his soul. He was happy, and also he was sad. He had nothing to cry about, but he was ready to cry. For what? His earlier love? The little princess? His disappointments? His hopes for the future? . . . Yes and no. The main thing that he wished to cry for was his sudden vivid awareness of the terrible contrast between something infinitely great and indefinable within him and something narrow and corporeal which he was himself and even she was. This contrast brought him distress and joy during her singing.

Again the response to the song has allowed Tolstoy to transform a conventional love scene into a searching examination of a complex of emotions.

Some time later the apparent superior naturalness of a Russian national life, uncontaminated by Western ways, is conveyed to Natasha during her visit to her uncle after the hunt, mainly through the music of balalaika and guitar, and the Russian dance, the instinctive movements for which had not been stifled by the *pas de châle*. It is this music that first causes doubts and worries about her relationship with Andrey to come to Natasha. Would *he* appreciate this music-making that she so enjoys? The refrain of that music, now linked with worrying thoughts about Andrey, re-echoes in the

Rostovs' drawing room. It is the picking out on her uncle's folk guitar of a phrase she had heard in a St Petersburg opera with Prince Andrey that ushers back first memories of her distant betrothed, and then, when she plays for Sonya, the despair at her enforced parting from him.

The examination of the love relationship between Andrey and Natasha continues with music. Even the mother's complicated response to her daughter's match is brought out by music. The mood of that scene is set by Dimmler playing Countess Rostova's favourite Field nocturne on the harp by moonlight (there is no indication that "European" music is any less potent than Russian folk music in its ability to promote the transference of thought and emotion). Then Natasha sings at the clavichord her mother's favourite song to the assembled gathering. Again it is the complexity of the listener's emotion, in this case, that of the old countess, that resonates to the formal song. Feelings are apprehended which could not be expressed in any conversation with her daughter or in cogitation.

> The old Countess sat with a happily melancholic smile and tears in her eyes, shaking her head from time to time. She thought of Natasha, and of her youth, and that there was something unnatural and frightful in Natasha's forthcoming marriage with Prince Andrey. . . . Her mother's intuition told her that Natasha had too much of something and consequently would not be happy.

The ominous feelings called forth by the resonance of the singing voice are interrupted by the sudden arrival of the domestics as mummers who launch into their traditional songs, dances, choruses and games. Drawing room music yields to the rude gaiety of folk traditions: yet the mumming provides the same type of artificial background fostering human intercourse as Field's nocturnes. The only difference is in a register of culture. Yet it is through these artificial conventions alone, however varied they may be, that Tolstoy informs his reader that men may communicate. Despite their living closely together, Nikolay had found it impossible to declare his love for Sonya. It is only when released by the grotesque artificiality of the mumming from their conventional selves that Nikolay, in an elderly lady's farthingale, and Sonya, as a moustachioed Circassian, seal their love with a kiss redolent of burnt cork from Sonya's mock moustache.

That their love was not expressed sufficiently in truth, but in the rigmarole of mumming, does of course suggest its instability. Yet the mumming is not treated by Tolstoy in as harsh a fashion as the rigmarole of sentimentalism through which Boris and Julie have to arrange their match. The sentimental verses with their melancholic descriptions of gloamings and graveyards, penned in Julie's album, the doleful nocturnes on the harp, the emotional reading of Karamzin's *Poor Liza* together, all necessary signals in Boris's plan to make a rich match—but the literature of sentimentalism had fooled neither Boris nor Julie. Whereas in the previous chapters artificialities had managed to crystallise human relationships which were dimly felt but had not found their expression, here there was an emotional emptiness between Boris and Julie that not even the heightened emotionality of a forced sentimentalism could fill. Despite the album verses and the harp's nocturnes, the marriage would remain one of cool convenience: "The betrothed, without further mention of the trees plunging them in gloom and melancholy, made plans for the future setting up of a splendid home in Petersburg, went visiting and made full preparation for a splendid wedding."

With the excesses of sentimental literature apparently mocked, it would not seem strange for Tolstoy to find operatic conventions more laughable. Towards the end of this volume, there is the passage describing Natasha's visit to the opera which has become a classical reference in Tolstoy criticism. Yet our response to that opera visit may be distorted if we peruse that performance in isolation from the preceding ones. The fresh young girl from the country is apparently made to see through artificial staginess.

> They all sang something. When they finished their song, the girl in white went up to the prompter's box and was approached by a man in tight silk trousers over his plump legs, with a plume and dagger who began to sing and wave his arms.
>
> The man in the tight trousers sang alone, then she sang. Then both fell silent, the music struck up and the man began to finger the arm of the girl in the white dress, evidently waiting for the beat again in order to begin a new duet with her. They sang together and everyone in the theatre clapped and shouted and the man and woman on the stage who represented lovers, took their bows, smiling and extending their arms.

The visit to the opera has often been quoted in support of the view that central to Tolstoy's method was *ostraneniye*, "estrangement" or "making strange," a term coined by Shklovsky to define Tolstoy's specific ironic detachment, a view as piercingly fresh as that of the boy who refused to see the Emperor's clothes. Yet here, it is not Tolstoy but Natasha who refuses to form the opera in her mind, from her perception of its conventions. There is no reason to suppose that Natasha was incapable of grasping the peculiarities of the opera: although fresh from the country, she had received voice training, had been credited by Dimmler with "a real European talent," and had lovingly recalled a visit to the opera in St Petersburg with Prince Andrey. What causes her to reject the opera is not so much its absurdity—if ironic detachment had been rigorously applied, the folksy balalaika strumming at the uncle's could be made equally absurd. Tolstoy does not grade the ritual ways of communication into ones which are more or less artificial, or more or less genuine. It is the reaction of the audience to performance that for him is crucial: a melancholy nocturne played at the Rostovs' can elicit real feelings, whereas the same nocturne played by Julie Karagina for Boris would echo in the emptiness of their relationship. The opera is another "performance" in the series of performances which have illuminated the variety of sexual bonding in this part of the novel. The description of the opera in that context is not intended mainly to show the absurdity of artifice, or the superiority of Natasha's naive vision. Her failure to take in the opera results from the cruel rebuff she has just experienced from the Bolkonskys and the impossibility of having any reassurance from the absent Andrey: her rejection by them is turned into her rejection of the opera. The highly-strung Natasha, put more on edge by the tension of the operatic event, becomes hysterical: "She looked and thought, and the strangest thoughts suddenly, without cause, flashed through her head. Now the thought presented itself of jumping behind the footlights to sing the aria which the *artiste* was singing, now she wanted to flick the old man sitting near her with her fan, lean over towards Hélène and tickle her." It is at this moment that Anatole Kuragin, her seducer, makes his appearance in the theatre: one might almost see it as a dramatic operatic entry. Motivating the seduction of Natasha by Anatole and making it plausible was undoubtedly difficult. Again though, as with all the other sexual bondings in this part of the novel, it is the ritual performance that acts as a catalyst: slowly Natasha begins to accommodate the conventions of the opera, and eventually as she begins to be fascinated by the male peacockery of Kuragin, she joins in the mass hysteria for the male dancer Dupport. That the final storm is an artificial creation of chromatic scales and diminished seventh chords is no longer a barrier: "Natasha no longer found it strange. She looked around her with pleasure and a joyful smile." By accepting the star performer, she had shown herself ready to accept Kuragin. And Natasha's new response to the final act is what informs us of the strength of the bond forged between her and Anatole Kuragin during the interval:

> Again the curtain rose. Anatole left the box composed and happy. Natasha returned to her father's box completely subject

to the world in which she found herself. Everything which took place before her already seemed completely natural; but on the other hand all her previous thoughts about her betrothed, Princess Marya, life in the country not once entered her head, as if all that was in the distant, distant past.

On the next occasion when Natasha meets Anatole at a soirée at Hélène's, it is again a performance, this time a declamation by Mademoiselle Georges of some French verse "about her criminal love for her son," presumably from *Phèdre,* that causes Natasha to return to the "strange, senseless world, so far removed from her previous one," where she is open to Anatole's advances. Finally the seduction is completed by Natasha's trusting acceptance of a letter from Anatole. From all the artful performances the reader has witnessed, the truthfulness of the written word, carefully weighed for the benefit of the audience—we may remember Natasha's own letters to Andrey written almost as school compositions with the spelling mistakes corrected by her mother—cannot be trusted. Ironically, Marya's sincere letter of apology to Natasha does not find any response in its addressee, rather as Pierre's honesty is invariably misunderstood. What Natasha accepts as the truth is a letter, apparently from a passionate lover, but in fact composed for Anatole by Dolokhov: yet it is in that sham that she finds "echoes of all that she thought she had felt herself." It is the literary fake that turns Natasha: " 'Yes, yes, I love him!'—thought Natasha rereading the letter for the twentieth time and searching for some special deep meaning in its every word."

From the above, we see that "performances" by their inherent fraudulence pervert human relationships and particularly sexual bondings. Honest, straightforward communication on the other hand—such as Pierre's address to his masonic lodge or Marya's letter to Natasha—do not find a receptive audience. For Tolstoy, communicability is possible only when narrator and listener both understand the futility of transferring thought and emotion through words alone. And of course, this is the accord that he would wish to make with his reader. Again such understandings, brought about by the recognition that full communication is not possible, occur at high points in the novel such as Andrey's recollection of a communion with Natasha on the eve of the Battle of Borodino. For Andrey to admit to such understanding is particularly remarkable since throughout the novel he is one who spurns vain attempts at relating experience from the moment when he shies away from the anecdotes in Anna Scherer's salon. He is the one who brings Nikolay's tale of Schöngraben to an end, and the most poignant example of his failure to relate to others through "performance" is his breaking off the tale of Bluebeard to his son. Yet on the eve of Borodino, unable to sleep, he remembers Natasha recounting the story of being lost in the forest while mushrooming. Exasperated by her apparent failure to tell her story, Natasha keeps explaining this to Andrey: "Natasha was not content with her words—she felt that the passionately poetic experience which she had felt that day and which she wished to bring to the surface was not coming out." Yet in her failure to tell it as it was, Natasha communicated with Andrey. He consequently understood and loved her. But the man of war only came to understand this as his final battle approached.

V

All these narratives and performances are, of course, enfolded within Tolstoy's own great narrative which holds forth to an audience in the same way. It is remarkable to find as the novel is brought to a resolution that the story of *War and Peace* is, as it were, retold within the novel. And it is retold through the mouth of Pierre who eventually is able, through the reprise, to achieve real communicability while preserving his honesty. Central to the resolution of the novel is the fact that the Pierre who, throughout the course of the novel found his rage for honesty an impediment to communication, is at last able to transfer his thoughts to another in his love for Natasha.

In the treatment of Pierre's realisation of his love for Natasha, Tolstoy demonstrated in a powerfully ironic way the force of an insincere tangential narrative in crystallising real emotions. Pierre's full understanding of his love comes when he acts as an audience to Captain Ramballe's risqué recital of his amorous adventures: nothing could be more absurd than that the tipsy captain's recital should bring Pierre to a realisation of love. Pierre reciprocates with a telling of his own story—which in a way is a retelling of the story that the readers of *War and Peace* know—and again Pierre fails to communicate. What Ramballe grasps as the main import is not the essence of Pierre's love for Natasha, but that he was rich with two palaces in Moscow. Ramballe is made to appear as a comically misunderstanding audience with which the reader of the novel can compare himself to his own advantage.

If his story told to Ramballe ends in a fiasco of non-comprehension, Pierre finally is able to achieve communication when in chapter 17 of the last volume he tells his story—again a reprise of what we have learnt from the novel itself—to Marya and Natasha. Pierre begins by giving expression to all those problems of evaluating experience and communicating it, which we have discussed: "I am told about such miracles which I have not dreamt of. Marya Abramovna invited me to her house and kept on telling me what happened to me or what should have happened. Stepan Stepanych also taught me how I should tell my stories." Repetition, as R. F. Christian has demonstrated, is one of Tolstoy's most powerful techniques, and this chapter reverberates with the repetition of the verb *rasskazyvat'* (to narrate) and its cognate noun *rasskaz*. Pierre is being importuned to tell a conventional story (what should have happened) in conventional terms (Stepan Stepanych taught me how I should tell my stories). But at last Pierre is able to turn away from self-mockery and tell of *real experiences* naturally; what had made his narrations so awkward previously, from the first one in Anna Scherer's salon, was that he had been only able to speak honestly of abstractions or, at best, of half-digested experiences. Now he began to speak "with the restrained enthusiasm of a man experiencing strong impressions in his recollections." Pierre at last understands that true communication, "man speaking to man," is akin to Wordsworth's celebrated understanding of poetry, originating in "emotion recollected in tranquillity . . . till by a species of reaction, all tranquillity gradually disappears, and an emotion, kindred to that which was before the subject of contemplation, is gradually produced and does itself actually exist in the mind." Again, of course, the act of narration, the "performance," marks a climactic moment in the novel. Whereas previously the performances were flawed and the accompanying sexual bondings insecure, finally, in the closure of *War and Peace*, we find that the union of Pierre and Natasha is made manifest by a perfected narration fused with a most sympathetic reception. What effects the union is not eloquence (even at this moment Tolstoy launched into a scathing aside at *intelligent* women who listen to words to retell them or to use them as starting points for their little "laboratorial" thoughts), but the whole narrating experience whose significance Pierre had grasped with Platon Karatayev whose stories were told with the naturalness of a singing bird.

And in this new-found way of telling, he finds his ideal listener in Natasha, who responds in the way that Tolstoy would probably have wished any reader of his to react. By look and gesture she indicates to him that "she understood exactly what he wished to transmit"; and more than that, "It was evident that she understood not only what he was telling but also what he would wish to tell but could not express in words." It is in the telling itself that Pierre became fully aware of the significance of experience—as Tolstoy himself had become aware of the significance of his own experiences during the long writing of *War and Peace*—and Natasha in her reaction personified the ideal reader that Tolstoy would have wished to reach out for: "Natasha, without knowing it, was all attention: she did not let slip a word, a tremor of the voice, a look, a shudder of a facial muscle, nor a gesture of Pierre's. She caught in flight the as yet unexpressed word and carried it straight into her open heart, guessing the secret significance of Pierre's whole spiritual world."

At the novel's end, having pleaded with his reader and hectored him, having shown him the futility of seeking to transmit experience, and the fluidity of human language, and having also demonstrated to him that only in his narrations and performances to his fellows could man hope to give form to his existence, Tolstoy too, through Pierre, rests content in the knowledge that in making *War and Peace*, he had also made his reader.

War and Peace:
The Theoretical Chapters

Edward Wasiolek

The point of the long theoretical discussion of history that dominates the later portions of *War and Peace* is to prove that necessity and freedom are resolved in the concrete historical act—the same point that Tolstoy has dramatized in the best moments of the domestic portions of the novel. Percy Lubbock was wrong when he said that Tolstoy was writing two novels without knowing it, and the Soviet critic Bocharov is right when he says that there is only one novel in *War and Peace,* and that the same laws govern both the movement of individuals and the movement of nations and historical events. Nowhere are the antinomies of freedom and necessity, which Tolstoy discusses at such length in the later chapters of *War and Peace,* and the resolution of these antinomies more eloquently communicated than in the hunt scene. The laws that Tolstoy formulates abstractly about freedom and necessity are the same that are shown to move the drama of the hunt.

Although we sense instinctively that the hunt scene is one of the high points of *War and Peace,* it is difficult to know why the hunt of the old grey wolf and its capture should be so moving. The scene has something of the impenetrability of Hemingway's *Big Two-Hearted River,* where one is exasperatingly in the presence of what seems to be a very special experience and vocabulary, and yet where one recognizes that something universal is being communicated. Hemingway's vocabulary of leaders, lines, strains, wet grasshoppers, and large trout is matched by the special vocabulary of

From *Tolstoy's Major Fiction.* © 1978 by the University of Chicago. University of Chicago Press, 1978.

the hunt with its special cries, terms for hounds, and elaborate rules. There can be no mistaking that this is one of Tolstoy's sacramental scenes. Tolstoy often signals such scenes by special images, such as the sky. Just as almost all of Andrey's "best moments" are signaled by a sky image, it is to the sky that Tolstoy draws our attention on the day of the hunt. We are told that there is a mist in the autumnal air and that the sky looks as if it is melting into microscopic drops of moisture, which are falling to the earth. Tolstoy pictures the sky as if it is touching the earth. He uses the same technique when Nikolay kisses Sonya in her mummer's costume; for an instant their tiresome love becomes true and vital, because the ever-same Sonya appears different in her costume to Nikolay. They kiss to the background of the sky touching the earth and of stars scattered in reflection on the snow. On the day of the hunt the twigs are covered with glistening drops of dew, just as a dew illuminated by moonlight signaled the special experience of Andrey's reaction to Natasha's excited voice at Otradnoe, and as a dew-illuminated garden signals the love and happiness flowing in both Sergey's and Masha's hearts in *Family Happiness*.

The enigmatic character of the hunt scene has led critics—when they have bothered to explain it at all—to symbolize and allegorize it. Bocharov, who has concerned himself with the inner relations of *War and Peace* more than any other Soviet critic, sees the scene as connected with the rest of *War and Peace*. But the only connection he makes is to read it as an allegory of the historical struggle of the people. The point is not as farfetched or as doctrinaire as it sounds, since Bocharov makes a good case of how "hunt" imagery permeates many scenes of heroism. Still, there is a considerable stretching in such an interpretation and, more important, very little explanation why "hunting," whether real or symbolic, should create such a beautiful experience. The feeling of beauty comes from our recognition that we are touching that inner circle where life beats in its plenitude—a recognition present in the best moments of *War and Peace*. What the hunt scene shows us in dramatic fashion is how it feels to live for oneself and at the same time for others, or how it feels to be free and determined at the same time.

The beginning of that confluence of freedom and necessity is seen in the decivilizing process that takes place in the preparations for the hunt. The usual patriarchal distinctions disappear, and a more primitive and natural order supplants them, an order that comes from the nature of the task and the circumstances before them. Danilo the serf gives the orders, and Ilya Rostov the master accepts them. The "primitivizing" of a scene is something that one would expect from Tolstoy, and it is something he has done and will do not only in the stag's lair scene in *The Cossacks* but also in *Master and Man* and in the mowing scene in *Anna Karenina*. The point is, of course, to regress from the excrescences of civilization, but it is not— as I have cautioned before—to recommend some uncivilized state as desirable. Tolstoy does not extol the noble savage. What follows the reversal of hierarchies is no immersion into "chaos" or "disorder"; rather, the scene is just as ordered, decorous, and ritualistic as a ball. What characterizes it is to a large extent the absence of anything arbitrary. There is the sense of everyone knowing his place and doing his job without command or coercion, almost silently, as if language were a social instrument that separated one from the immediate experience. Tolstoy often signals the importance of an experience by the half-disappearance of normal discourse, as if such discourse were an obstacle to true communication. The asseverations of love of Sergey and Masha in *Family Happiness* and of Kitty and Levin in *Anna Karenina* take place with abbreviated language. There and here Tolstoy wants to convey the sense of things taking place by themselves. "Every dog knew its master and its call. Every man in the hunt knew his task, his place, and the part assigned him. As soon as they had passed beyond the fence, they all moved without noise or talk, lengthening out along the road and the field to the Otradnoe forest."

What Tolstoy is attempting to describe is how it feels to be personally and intensely absorbed in an experience and yet to be part of a group. Nikolay and others are doing what they want to do; yet what they want is what others want and what the circumstances necessitate. Tolstoy is describing a free necessity, which is an at-one-ness not only between the individual and others but also between the inside of the individual and the circumstances he finds himself in. When this happens to Nikolay, he experiences one of the happiest moments of his life. And it happens when he catches sight of the old wolf. This moment is expressed in the Garnett translation in this way: "A stroke of great good fortune had come to him, and so simply, without noise, or flourish, or display to signalize it." In the Russian, "Sovershilos' velichayshee shchast'e—i tak prosto, bez shuma, bez bleska, bez oznamenovaniya," the word *shchast'e* means both "happiness" and "luck." Although "happiness" is probably the better translation, the word has something of the "unintendedness" that "luck" signals in English. The word *shum* is literally "noise," but it is probably being used here in the sense of "trouble" or "commotion," since Tolstoy wants to convey the ease with which the moment appears. The happiness comes by itself; it is not planned, caused, or coerced. It is simple and natural and it does not draw attention to itself (*bez bleska*). Nikolay ardently wishes the wolf to appear, but when it appears, there is no distance between wish and reality. They are one; the tension is gone, the distance is closed, and there is no inner and outer. The wolf in Nikolay's prayers and wishes is the wolf in his perception. But it is one thing to show such a confluence of necessity and freedom and another to explain it, and this is what Tolstoy attempts to do in his much-discussed and much-criticized theoretical chapters.

In the philosophical chapters Tolstoy attempts to explain what he means by freedom and necessity, and he does so with a language that becomes more and more abstract and more and more remote from the dramatic portions of the novel. As a consequence these philosophical chapters have been universally belabored. An early Russian critic called them "disgusting"; Turgenev found them wearisome; Flaubert threw up his hands in consternation; Lubbock spoke of a theory drummed into the reader with merciless iteration, "desolating many a weary page"; Janko Lavrin spoke of the history as "encumbering the narrative to the point of weariness"; and for Noyes the chapters were a blemish and the theory "of no importance except as coming from Tolstoy." A year after the first French translation of *War and Peace* appeared (in 1874), C. Courrière wrote what was to be a characteristic comment: "Why is it that the admiration one feels for something so beautiful must be ruined by the philosophical theories of the author? In this gigantic struggle between two worlds and in this great displacement of humanity, Count Tolstoy has seen only a conjunction and series of accidental causes having nothing to do with human will. Napoleon, Alexander, Kutuzov, Bagration, and the French and the Russians are mere pawns on a huge chessboard moved by the hand of destiny. The author's fatalism is argumentative and doctrinaire; it reduces all the great events of the age to its small measure."

The chapters have had few defenders, but Tolstoy himself defended his views as serious and important. In the rough drafts of the novel, Tolstoy says of his views on history, "What I have expressed in the epilogue of the novel, without quotations and references, is not the momentary fancy of my mind but the inevitable conclusions of seven years of work, which I had to do." After publication he wrote in somewhat the same vein to Pogodin: "My thoughts about the limits of freedom and necessity and my view of history are not chance paradoxes, which I have taken up for the moment. These thoughts are the fruit of all my mental labor of life, and they constitute an inseparable part of that world view, which God knows with what labor and suffering I worked out and which has given me complete peace and happiness. Nevertheless, I know and knew that the tender scenes about young girls, the satire of Speransky, and trifles of that kind would be praised, because people are capable of understanding only those things. But no one will take notice of what is important." There is something spiteful and something of injured pride in these remarks. We need not, however, agree with him that his descriptions of "young girls" are trivial, and we can still grant him that his thoughts on freedom and necessity have not been taken seriously enough.

His position on history has been reduced to the antiheroic view of history, and his philosophical position on free will and necessity has been reduced to something that has ordinarily been called *fatalism* or determinism, which in Western tradition suggests a view of the world like Calvin's or Zola's. Some of this may have been fostered by mistranslation, since Garnett uses the word "determinism" many times when Tolstoy says something else, and usually at crucial junctures. Here is one example. According to Garnett, Tolstoy says of Napoleon, "In both cases his personal activity having no more force than the personal activity of every soldier was merely coincidental with the laws by which the event was determined." What Tolstoy was really saying was, "the laws by which the event was accomplished."

The word "fatalism" used to describe Tolstoy's theory of history has not left the lips of critics from the time of publication until today. The critic Akhsharumov accused Tolstoy of fatalism shortly after publication of the chapters; Courrière spoke of "doctrinaire fatalism": Noyes spoke of "blind fatalism" and so on. Yet Tolstoy said of fatalism: "Fatalism for man is just as foolish as free will in historical events." Isaiah Berlin assumes with others that Tolstoy believed in a thoroughgoing determinism and looked on free will as an illusion. Berlin's remarks on fatalism and determinism are not, as in the case of the other critics, a casual judgment but are a thoroughgoing consideration of the implications of freedom and determinism for the structure and coherence of the novel. If Berlin is right—that a thoroughgoing determinism informs Tolstoy's remarks in the philosophical chapters—then there exists an irreconcilable dilemma at the core of Tolstoy's thought and art.

The dilemma is this: all the variegated inner and outer life that Tolstoy traces with such unsurpassed accuracy, fullness, and freshness is nevertheless "illusion" because such life presupposes moral consciousness and moral consciousness presupposes free will, and Tolstoy exposes tenaciously and repeatedly the illusion of free will. Here is one of Berlin's many statements of this central theme:

> On the one hand, if those feelings and immediate experiences, upon which the ordinary values of private individuals and historians alike ultimately rest, are nothing but a vast illusion, this

must in the name of truth, be ruthlessly demonstrated, and the values and the explanations which derive from the illusion exposed and discredited. And in a sense Tolstoy does try to do this, particularly when he is philosophizing, as in the great public scenes of the novel itself, the battle pieces, the descriptions of the movements of peoples, the metaphysical disquisitions. But, on the other hand, he also does the exact opposite of this when he contrasts with this panorama of public life the superior value of personal experience, the "thoughts, knowledge, poetry, music, love, friendship, hates, passions of which real life is compounded"—when he contrasts the concrete and multi-coloured reality of individual lives with the pale abstractions of scientists or historians, particularly the latter, "from Gibbon to Buckle," whom he denounces so harshly for mistaking their own empty categories for real facts. And yet the primacy of these private experiences and relationships and virtues presupposes that vision of life, with its sense of personal responsibility, and belief in freedom and possibility of spontaneous action, to which the best pages of *War and Peace* are devoted, and which is the very illusion to be exorcized, if the truth is to be faced.

Berlin adds, "This terrible dilemma is never finally resolved." He assumes that the vividness, variety, and dramatic intensity of characters and scenes depend upon the presence of moral consciousness, that there is no moral consciousness without free will, and that Tolstoy demonstrated repeatedly that there is no free will. The reader may question Berlin's assumption that no moral consciousness is possible without free will, but the assumption is, I believe, valid. The difficulty does not lie there.

It is true that Tolstoy rails against the "great man" theory of history and against the view that men have the freedom to move historical events. It is equally true that he speaks of events and the lives of men as governed by law and necessity: Napoleon's fleeing army carries within itself—like a melting snowball—the elements of dissolution; the Russian retreat to the advantageous position at Tarutino takes place "by itself," that is, an army in retreat will necessarily follow its sources of supply, no matter what is decreed; the burning of Moscow is "bound to take place," given an abandoned city with a preponderance of wooden structures and the presence of an undisciplined, marauding army. But if Tolstoy believes in a thoroughgoing determinism, what does he mean by *free* when he says, in *War and Peace,* "An innumerable collection of freely acting forces (and nowhere is man freer than on the field of battle, where it is a question of life and death) influences the direction taken by a battle, and that direction can never be known before hand and never corresponds with the direction of any one force"? What does he mean, too, by his repeated statements in the notes and rough drafts that man is free and that "Eastern fatalism" is nonsense? Tolstoy believes in some kind of law of necessity, but this law does not exclude a limited freedom. Here is one of many formulations to be found in the rough drafts: "Our view not only does not exclude freedom but necessarily establishes its existence, based not on reason but on immediate consciousness. Whatever might be the general laws governing the world and man, the infinitely small moment of freedom always is inseparably part of me." But what is this freedom which is not excluded by laws of necessity?

It is not the freedom to move events. Tolstoy's argument against heroes as the movers of history is merely a special instance of the broader proposition that no one has the freedom to move history. In order for a person to "cause" history, the event has to begin with him. He would have to step out of space and time, and God alone can do this. Everyone lives in time and space, and everyone lives in history and never outside it. An act of will which is not conditioned by anything outside itself is an abstraction and hence unreal. It is an illusion, as is the belief of generals that they can direct the course of battles, and as are all those individual acts of the dramatic sections of the novel which are based on th premise that one knows what is going to happen.

If no one, then, has the freedom to initiate events, who or what causes events? According to Tolstoy, everyone and everything participating in the event causes the event. All the forces and conditions, both inner and outer, that are part of the event cause the event. Result y, then, is not caused by x or by x^2 or x^3 but by x^n. Tolstoy states his views on this point with uncompromising repetition throughout the theoretical chapters: "If many forces are acting simultaneously in different directions on any body, the direction of its motion will not correspond with any one of the forces, but will always follow a middle course, the summary of them, what is expressed in mechanics by the diagonal of the parallelogram of forces. . . . To find the component forces that make up the composite or resultant force it is essential that the sum of the component parts should equal the resultant. . . . The only conception by means of which the movements of nations can be explained is a conception of a force equal to the whole movement of nations."

We seem to be back with the necessity that we have denied. Men do not cause events by their wills but are themselves caused by the totality of conditions that are part of the event. Is this not a thoroughgoing determinism? Even more, Tolstoy devotes considerable attention to the possibilities of discovering the laws that govern the emergence and operation of historical events, a concern that would seem to reemphasize his belief in the normative and hence unfree nature of events. His assumption that events are governed by laws and that these laws are at least partially discernible would seem to support all those who, like Berlin, have insisted that "fatalism" or "thoroughgoing determinism" best describe Tolstoy's view of history.

Reason is apparently capable of perceiving and formulating, at least in part, what is governed by laws. It is presumably the incalculable complexity of those laws that prevents us from understanding how an event will take place. If the world is governed by laws and men have a faculty by which the laws may be discerned, then it is reasonable to expect—no matter how elementary man's knowledge may be at the present time—that men will eventually understand fully the laws that govern phenomena. Theoretically, this would seem to follow even though practically it might be impossible. It was this consideration that led Berlin to hypothesize that by some incredible calculus men might theoretically understand the laws that govern history.

Nevertheless, Tolstoy expresses unmitigated scorn for those who attempt rationally to discern the laws that govern phenomena. His most bitter satire, after all, is reserved for the military leaders who believe that they can formulate the laws of battle and predict the course of a battle. Similarly, Tolstoy turns scathingly on those practitioners of science who look upon life only from the point of view of reason, find no place for free will, and believe that "the life of man is expressed in muscular movements that are conditioned by nervous activity." On one hand Tolstoy leads us to believe that the world is governed by laws which are at least potentially discernible by reason, and on the other hand he is bitterly critical of all attempts—in both theoretical and dramatic chapters—to discern and formulate those laws. Can man, by the use of reason, discern the laws that govern historical change or not? Tolstoy seems to give different and contradictory answers.

While seemingly championing the belief that laws governing historical phenomena exist, and even encouraging their discernment, Tolstoy is scornful of all efforts to predict events. It would seem that only ignorance prevents us from knowing the laws that govern phenomena. Once known, the laws must hold for all phenomena whether past, present, or future. Yet it is clear, without the slightest laboring, that Tolstoy, in both theory and drama, is uncompromising in his scorn for those who believe that they can predict events. His argument is as follows: Men cannot predict events because they live in time, space, and circumstance. An individual will always see event *x* from his point in time, space, and circumstance *y,* and the direction of *x* can be understood only when it is seen in the whole series of events of which it is a part. Tolstoy puts it this way: "Only the expression of the Will of the Deity, not depending on time, can relate to a whole series of events that have to take place during several years or centuries; and only the Deity, acting by his will alone, not affected by any cause, can determine the direction of the movement of humanity. Man acts in time, and himself takes part in the event." Tolstoy seems to believe in strict historical limitation of view, and it is this belief that moves him to look with contempt upon those historians who attempt to arraign history. Those who criticized Alexander's actions fifty years later and accused him of reactionary politics argued nonsensically that history should have been something other than it was and that they had an invariable measure by which to judge Alexander's acts. Alexander did, Tolstoy tells us, what the times and his nature demanded. There is no such thing as good or bad history and no measure by which historical personages may be tried.

Still, if our strictly limited point of view and consequent inability to understand the direction of events explain why we cannot predict the operation of the laws that govern phenomena, it would seem that the same strict historical limitation would prevent us from discerning and understanding any laws. Yet in other arguments Tolstoy seems to assume that men can discern and understand these laws. One can summarize the difficulties encountered thus far in this way: Tolstoy tells us that "free will" is an illusion as we commonly conceive of it, but he tells us man is "freer" in some conditions than in others and that he always has some irreducible element of freedom as part of his nature. Events are governed by laws, and it is within the cognizance of man to discern these laws, but those who attempt to discern them—generals, men of science, historians—are idiots. Man is strictly limited by his "historicity" and cannot step out of history to judge it. In short, man is free and he is not free; laws govern and do not govern history.

At this point we can dismiss his theory of history as nonsense—and some have done this—or we can disregard contravening evidence and choose either necessity or freedom for Tolstoy. When this has been done— Isaiah Berlin has done it—the choice has been made, almost without exception, for thoroughgoing determinism. Yet it is impossible to choose determinism for Tolstoy since he himself explicitly denies it in the very chapters under discussion. Tolstoy says: "But in neither case, however we shift our point of view, however clear we make to ourselves the connection in which man is placed with the external world, or however fully comprehensible it may appear to us, however long or short a period of time we select, however explicable or unfathomable the causes of the act may be to us, we can never conceive of complete free will, nor of complete necessity in any action."

Could there be a more direct, explicit refutation? How is it possible—in the face of such a statement—that distinguished critics have for so long insisted that Tolstoy believed in determinism? It can only be that they disregard or reject what Tolstoy says in support of freedom and accept for personal reasons what he has to say about necessity. The answer to these puzzles lies, I believe, in a set of crucial definitions Tolstoy makes. I am referring to Tolstoy's extended definition of the two faculties of man, reason and consciousness (*soznanie*). The correct understanding of these two terms will permit us to know how man can be free and yet unfree, bound by necessity and yet free of necessity. And it will permit us to dispel the dilemma that Isaiah Berlin has found to lie at the core of *War and Peace*. The word *soznanie* might also be translated by "experience" or "awareness." Since the English word "consciousness" is not sufficiently differentiated from "rational process," the crucial opposition between these two modes of cognition is obscured. The French word *conscience* is better translation. The constituent parts of the Russian word are the morpheme *so* and the radical *znanie* (knowledge). The force of the morpheme *so* is that of "withness" or "linkage," and one might conceive of the meaning of the word as knowledge attended by being *with* or *at one with* the object of cognition. The fact that English slang has evolved the expression of being "with" something may be testimony to the lack of such a concept in standard English.

Consciousness (*soznanie*), then, is a form of knowledge or awareness radically different from rational knowledge. "Consciousness" is immediate, personal, present, and experiential. Reason is abstract, general, and impersonal. For consciousness the world is "subject," for reason it is "object" (*predmet*). Garnett translates *predmet* as subject and confuses the whole opposition. Reason denies the freedom of man; consciousness affirms it. The opposition between the two is complete and unqualified, and Tolstoy tells us that it is impossible to affirm which is true. The last point is the most important, because, if we accept the evidence of reason, there cannot be a single instance of free will; everything is governed by laws. If we accept the evidence of reason! But there is no indication that Tolstoy sees the evidence of reason as real and the evidence of consciousness as illusory, no indication that determinism was real and freedom illusory. There are considerable and explicit indications to the contrary. Tolstoy is at pains to deny that one can affirm one to be true and the other to be false. In the rough drafts of *War and Peace* he says: "The consciousness that I am free is a consciousness that cannot be proved and cannot be disproved by reason." To reason, the evidence of consciousness is wholly false; but to consciousness, the evidence of reason is wholly false. If Isaiah Berlin chose between the two, Tolstoy did not.

In the face of Tolstoy's repeated statements both in the text of the novel and in the rough drafts that neither reason nor consciousness are by themselves true and that man is free and he is bound, we can accept his discussion of the rational discernment of the laws of history only hypothetically. But if both reason and consciousness, necessity and freedom, are hypotheses and Tolstoy does not choose between them, does he then leave us with a dilemma that he refuses to resolve? Are we left with a choice, but no underpinnings for the choice, an either-or but no firm indication that one or the other is right? Such an unresolved formulation of the claims of necessity and freedom would be a more accurate assessment of Tolstoy's view of the problem than the categorical choice that Berlin and others have made in favor of reason and a consequent determinism. Yet Tolstoy has, I am convinced, resolved the problem, but has done so by denying the opposition of reason and consciousness and substituting for that opposition another one: reality and unreality. Both necessity and freedom are "unreal" and both are "real." They are unreal when each is asserted to be exclusively true.

The totally free choice assumes that the individual can step out of the nexus of space and time and initiate an act abstractly; the totally rational view of the world assumes that men can step out of space and time and conceive of the whole series of events. In both, man plays at being God. In both the world is turned into an object, for the abstract "free will" treats the world outside itself as an object just as surely as does the absolute reason. Total freedom and total necessity meet. The real act, however, cannot be either, for man does not live outside of history, but in history. Since he lives in history, he cannot step out of history to initiate events (unreal freedom), nor can he step out of history to judge history (unreal necessity). Those who attempt to command and those who attempt to arraign history are fools. They are foolish because one can know—really know—only one's own point in time and space. The more limited man becomes, the more real he becomes and the more effective he becomes in discerning the direction of reality. Paradoxically, a restriction of one's acts and one's view of events is really a widening of one's power over events. If the reasoning behind such a view is not immediately evident, it is clear that Tolstoy dramatizes such a situation again and again in the dramatic portions of *War and Peace*. It is Tushin, the obscure battery commander, and not Bagration the general who "moves" and "effects" events at the battle of Schongraben; it is the anonymous people who, giving no thought to the salvation of Russia but only to their private interests, save Russia. Personal acts and not public concerns move history because they are real acts, being responses to immediate circumstances and immediate time; public concerns exceed in their generality what one is immediately in touch with. One cannot "freely" move history, but one can move freely in history by responding to the actual events one finds oneself in.

If one conceives of real history as a nexus of conditions that are constantly changing, and if one accepts the fact that one's experience of such reality is restricted to one coordinate of that changing nexus, then it is clear that one will be closer to the actual movement of reality to the extent that one is responding to what is before one immediately. To the extent that one reflects, feels, and chooses on the basis of past moments or imagined future moments, or on the basis of abstractions that presumably hold for all moments, one will be at a remove from the real and ever-changing flow of circumstances. That is, one's choices will be based on illusion and not on reality. One will be most effective to the extent that one is most in touch with reality, that is, in touch with what is before one, what is outside one and inside one at any particular moment. Both "determinism" and "free will" are abstractions when they are held above the flow of actual and ever-changing circumstances. This is no different from what Tolstoy dramatizes in the novel. The Teutonic generals believe that they can predict what will happen, when according to Tolstoy one can know only what is happening and then only what is happening to oneself at a particular moment and in a particular place. This is why their scratchings on the blackboard are unreal and their commands are so much at variance with what actually happens. The finished products of society, such as Prince Vassily and Anna Pavlovna Scherer, are shown to behave like marionettes because they have removed themselves from actual reality by the regularity and predictive quality of the conventions they live by, which are always the same and consequently always at variance with changing circumstances. Natasha is in touch with real life at the ball because she attends to what is at hand and acknowledges the feelings she actually experiences as they are called for by the circumstances about her. She has immersed herself in herself, that is, in what she is actually in touch with. Platon Karataev, it will be remembered, is so much at one with what is before him that he forgets a thing or a person—even a good friend—that is no longer before him.

If we try to understand Tolstoy's real "necessity" without reference to a supernatural force, it must be something like this: man is limited by everything about him, but most of all by other people. Like a rolling sphere, he can go only a short distance without being deflected from the original direction by others. What limits him are the choices of other people. Other people are his necessity. A historical event is bound to be, not because of a law above the choices of people, but because a great number of people influenced by numberless conditions, inner and outer, create an event *x*. The choices create the event, not the event the choices. If we ask the classic question of whether or not the result could have been different, we ask something that cannot be answered, because history cannot be retried, or because, as Tolstoy says in the rough drafts, history is no longer history when we ask that question, but is rather the concept of history. The necessity of history may be indifferent to individual choice, but not to individual choices. Necessity is reality, that is, the compound of real life, the result of numberless choices, themselves influenced by numberless choices before them. One's free act contributes to necessity, and the totality of free acts is necessity. Freedom is necessity, and necessity is freedom.

The phrase "result of free choices" is important because it explains why Tolstoy can insist on "free choice" as an inevitable element in every historical act, and can also discuss the "laws" of history and their disengagement, while condemning every act of prediction. What has happened is different from what is taking place. Freedom is possible only in what is taking place; it does not exist in what has taken place. These are not my paradoxes. They are Tolstoy's: "The consciousness that I am free is consciousness and cannot be proved or disproved by reason; but the consciousness that I *was* free is a concept and therefore amenable to reason. If a man says: I know that I was free, he states a conclusion. I am free in the present moment; the past was present at the moment when I accomplished my act, and I was consequently free and I could consequently act as I did or differently." What has happened has happened necessarily (as a consequence of free choice) and is consequently amenable to reason and to partial discernment of laws governing the events. These laws must be purely descriptive, however, and cannot be true universals that have predictive power. They are the consequences of free choices and not the determiners of free choice. Individual freedom, however, is always freedom qualified and conditioned by other free choices, and ultimately by the totality of free choices. Such conditioned and limited freedom is never perceived by reason and is always perceived by consciousness.

We can now understand why both in drama and in theory the sacramental moments are always individual, immediate, and in some special way "free." Freedom and necessity meet in the individual act, and only in the truly individual act. The more immediate, concrete, and individual the consciousness, the richer, fuller, and freer is the consciousness. These are more than paradoxes. One becomes conscious of the world to the extent that one permits it to rise in one's consciousness, and one permits it to rise in one's consciousness to the extent that one withdraws one's control over the world, whether the control is one of command, judgment, wish, hope, grief, or countless other subjective acts and impulses. True freedom then is for Tolstoy not the power to initiate events abstractly, as if one were exempt from space and time and from preceding conditions, but the consciousness of reality. The fuller and richer the consciousness (*soznanie*), the freer one is. Such a conception of freedom will appear strange only if one judges it from what is for Tolstoy the unreal conception of freedom as the initiation of events. Natasha is "free" at the ball because she experiences concretely and immediately what is going on inside and outside her, not because she makes some "free" choice. Her freedom is the richness and plenitude of consciousness, that is, the immediate experience of much reality. It is "freedom" in that she is not the captive of any moment of the past or future, nor of the fixities of grief, hope, longing. Her immersion in self is a repossession of self in its concrete and tactile relationship with everything about her. This is a kind of freedom one feels when one is most "alive" and most at one with oneself.

The more individuality, the more reality. The very pivot of Tolstoy's theory of history is the individuality of people and the concreteness of history. In the face of this it is something of a shock to read in Kareev's full, and presumably authoritative, study of Tolstoy's theory of history the following: "The whole philosophy of history of *War and Peace* in actuality comes down to denying the role of individuality and individual initiative in history: history for Tolstoy is mass movement, which takes place in a fatalistic way, and great people are only the tag ends of history." Nothing could be more grievously wrong; no misunderstanding of Tolstoy's theory of history could be more resounding in its consequences. It is easy to see what led Kareev to such a misunderstanding, for the error is analogous to Berlin's misunderstanding: Kareev sees that Tolstoy rejects individual freedom of will in the sense of initiating and moving events and fails to see that Tolstoy formulates another kind of individual freedom as the very pivot of his interpretation of history.

The theoretical chapters of *War and Peace* deepen our understanding of the logic that runs through the motivation of the dramatic chapters and they imply and are implied by those chapters. It may seem to be a long way from the palpitation of Natasha's breast, the stumblings of Pierre, or the polished repartee of Prince Vassily and Anna Pavlovna to the discussion of history and the limits of free will and necessity, but the distance has been traversed by Tolstoy. Tolstoy's dramatic denigration of Napoleon, the tsar, and most military commanders finds its theoretical analogue in his arguments against the "great man" theory of history and in his argument against a certain kind of free will. In theoretical chapters he says that man is not free to step out of history and make reality. He says the same thing in the dramatic portions, and explores there the psychological consequences of believing in illusory freedom. He is concerned in the dramatic portions with how the belief in the illusion makes life sterile, and with great numbers of ways by which men attempt to impose their will on reality. The ends that the lives of men serve, Tolstoy states in both theory and drama, are incomprehensible. In the drama he shows how the intentions, fears, expectations, and plans of men are defeated by a logic that is greater and more complex than their efforts at understanding. In the theory, this thesis is limited to the impossibility of man's judging history or formulating predictive laws.

In both theory and drama, life beats with real rhythm when it is not abstract, that is, when it is not obscured by illusory freedom or by illusory necessity, but when it is personal, immediate, and full. Neither Natasha at the ball nor Pierre after prison nor Nikolay at the hunt nor Andrey before the oak command, predict, generalize, or anticipate life. One is most free when one is most personal and most immediate, in Tolstoy's radical sense, because it is only then that one has given up the wrong freedom of commanding life and has permitted the world in all its complexity to arise in one's consciousness. One possesses the world by giving it up. By becoming oneself, the individual permits the world to be itself. One cannot predict events, but if, like Kutuzov, one permits them to be, their manifold relationships—at least as they are being made—rise in one's consciousness, and the shape of these relationships may be known to a limited extent.

Isaiah Berlin's dilemma does not hold for *War and Peace.* Berlin and Tolstoy make different assumptions about freedom. Berlin is wrong in giving Tolstoy a conflict and a muddle that he never had. Tolstoy knew what he was doing; he knew he was denying "free will" both in theory and in drama and at the same time dramatizing characters that were living and free. Berlin assumes that Tolstoy could have drawn the data of experience so vividly only if the characters were "free," understanding by "free" the freedom to choose what life will be. Tolstoy believed that such freedom impoverishes life and that his characters could live fully only when they gave up the freedom to choose what life should be and accepted the freedom to let life be what it is. Berlin fails to see what Tolstoy repeats more than once: the world is not governed by the iron laws of necessity; man *is* free. He fails to see that Tolstoy condemns one kind of freedom and extols another; condemns one kind of necessity and extols another. Natasha, Pierre, Andrey, Nikolay, and the variety and vitality of Tolstoy's world are not contradicted by Tolstoy's theories. Berlin's dilemma exists in *The Hedgehog and the Fox,* but it does not exist in *War and Peace.*

What Tolstoy had sought since *Childhood* he found, or thought he found, and he dramatized it magnificently. The last leaf of the onion was unpealed; the golden kernel was found. No terror of vacuity confronted him; there was a measure at the center of the universe, and life beat full. The dream Tolstoy had in the early diaries—the dream of ease and beauty and of a world that unfolded by itself and in which men were at one with themselves and the world about them—is realized in *War and Peace.* Men need not be in disharmony with the world. The physical processes that work silently in distant galaxies work too in the spiritual and emotional chemistry of the inner man. There are no existential voids for Tolstoy, but there is in the objectivity of those inner and outer laws a distance and impersonality that must give one pause. The indifference of the laws is masked by the intensity of the senses and the vitalities of youth and un-masked by the weakening of the senses. It is the reality of those processes, indifferent to consciousness and the human element in the universe, that is discovered, confronted, and struggled with in *Anna Karenina.*

Anna Karenina and *War and Peace* are two worlds, and only their great-ness is similar. One is a culmination, the other a beginning. But that be-ginning is also an end. Tolstoy's conversion, the ten-year hiatus in creative writing, his preparations for martyrdom and his assumption of that role, the obsessions with sex and death which characterize all his later works— all these follow upon *Anna Karenina,* for the novel is already a harbinger of those momentous changes. Something light and happy goes out of his work and his life when we pass from *War and Peace* to *Anna Karenina.* No two novels could be more different. *War and Peace* is large and spacious, multicentered and man-centered. Men are in control. *Anna Karenina* is intense, focused in vision, and revealing of something dark and demonic in life. Men are not in control.

The Recuperative Powers of Memory: Tolstoy's *War and Peace*

Patricia Carden

The first intimation that *War and Peace* (*Voina i mir*) is on the horizon occurs in a letter Tolstoy writes to his sister-in-law in October 1862: "I am drawn now to leisurely work *de longue haleine*—a novel or something of the sort." By October of the next year work on the novel is under way, and Tolstoy writes confidently to his relative Alexandra Tolstoy, "I have never felt my intellectual and even all my moral forces so free and so ready for work. And I have that work. That work is a novel from the period of the 1810s and 20s, which has occupied me entirely since autumn. . . . I am now a writer with all the powers of my soul and I write and think as I never wrote and thought before." In letters to his friends and acquaintances the phrase "a long novel" recurs, for example, to Borisov, "I spend all my time writing a long novel, which I will finish only if I live a long time." A long breath, a long life, a long novel—these become interchangeable in Tolstoy's thinking in 1862 and 1863.

Finding a task that will sustain and extend his powers is a godsend to Tolstoy. Throughout the year in which he conceives and begins work on *War and Peace* he is troubled by fear of dissolution and mortality. "I thought that I had no strong interests or passions (how not have? why not have?)," he writes in his diary. "I thought that I was getting old and I was dying; I thought that it was terrible that I was not in love. I was horrified at myself because my interests were money and vulgar well-being. That was a periodic sleep. It seems to me that I have awakened." But he returns to his

From *The Russian Novel from Pushkin to Pasternak*, edited by John Garrard. © 1983 by Yale University. Yale University Press, 1983.

condition of torment and doubt and within months is writing in his diary, "I am horribly dissatisfied with myself. I reel and reel under the load of death and barely feel strength in myself to put a stop to it. But I don't want death, I want and love immortality. There's no point in choosing. The choice was made long ago. Literature, art, pedagogy and the family." This within days of boasting to Alexandra Tolstoy of his intellectual and moral powers. Escaping the burden of mortality becomes intimately tied up with writing the novel. Thus Tolstoy embarks upon his great meditation upon the powers that sustain life and hold death at bay. He is thirty-five years old and the task will occupy the next seven years of his life.

A novel "de longue haleine" "from the epoch of the 1810s and 20s" implies a sustained retrospective movement. It will of necessity be dependent upon the collective operation of memory that forms history. In fact, Tolstoy prepared himself to write the book by gathering up all the histories and memoirs of 1812 that he could lay hands upon. He engaged many people in the task of collecting materials, among them his sister-in-law Elizabeth, whom he instructed to find accounts of the daily life of the epoch. In his use of history and memoirs Tolstoy consistently chose the concrete and anecdotal, preferring memory functioning in its immediacy to the theorizing and organizing faculties of historians.

Memory was also to provide the basic stuff of plot. At the heart of *War and Peace* is the imagined world of the past at Yasnaya Polyana, Tolstoy's family home. He peoples his novel with the members of his family in the two previous generations, beginning with his father and his mother, who figure in the novel under their own names of Maria and Nikolai, and continuing back into the generation of the grandparents. The two principal families of the novel, the Rostovs and the Bolkonskys, transparently recreate the characters and conditions of life of the Tolstoys and Volkonskys, though Tolstoy has preserved his author's license to change much and even to add fictional characters to the families. The two family traditions are swelled out by the girlhood reminiscences of Tolstoy's wife and her sisters and by Tolstoy's own memories of childhood, youth, and military service. Memory, then, operating on many levels, collectively in the retrieved national experience, as family tradition, and in the immediacy of recollected personal experience, was to be the primary instrument for constructing the novel.

Yet memory was more to Tolstoy than the instrument he used to recover his materials. He had steeped himself in the texts of a philosophical tradition from Plato to the German idealists that made memory the keystone to the coherence of reality. At every stage in the constructing of the novel, he turned to a web of assumptions that were the very philosophical ground of his being, as natural to him as breathing. The argument for the primacy of memory, elaborated from Platonic doctrine, may be stated as follows: Memory guarantees the continuity of human experience against the dissolution imposed by temporal flux, which separates our every moment of experience from every other. Through the work of memory we retrieve and make present to ourselves the whole of our experience. Not only is memory capable of binding together that which seems disparate and discontinous in our earthly lives, not only is it the very basis of our sense of a coherent self, but it provides the most powerful argument for immortality of the soul. Since we seem to hold notions like "immortality of the soul" and "afterlife," where can we have gotten them if not through the operation of memory, for how could we conceive ideas of which we have no previous knowledge? When Western thought has moved toward rationalism, and our sense of a possible immortality has required explanation, memory has been called upon to supply the plausible ground for our expectation that after death we will go on to a higher world. The metaphysical model is based on operations of the mind: if memory can make present to us that which is absent, then cannot we apprehend a higher reality that cannot be made present to the senses? Memory proves to us every day the existence of a reality not evident to the senses.

The doctrine of memory appears explicitly in the text of *War and Peace* in a curious form. Its basic provisions are laid out in a conversation among the young people of the Rostov household during the winter spent in 1811 at Otradnoe, and the exponent is, unlikely as it seems, Natasha. Nikolai, Natasha, and Sonya have gathered casually in the sitting room and begin reminiscing about their shared childhood. Their conversation leads to more abstract, speculative considerations, such as whether we have recollection of past lives and what these past lives might have been. They come at last to discussion of the immortality of the soul.

Natasha begins the colloquy with a question couched in a language strikingly commonplace, wholly devoid of any suggestion of the metaphysical or even the philosophical. "Does it sometimes happen to you . . . that it seems to you that there's nothing more to come—nothing; that everything good has already been? And it's not so much boring, as sad?" Nikolai answers in like manner, confirming that the same feelings have recurred to him (*byvalo*). The confirmation as well as the reiterative form of the verb used by both speakers asserts a norm of human experience. We are alerted to Tolstoy's intention to develop the philosophical point of view directly from shared feeling rather than from abstract argument. This is the axiomatic ground of the philosophical dialogue that is to follow.

Though the exchange among the young people is at first confined to trivial memories of childhood, when the music master Dimmler approaches them, saying, "How quiet you young people are!" Natasha responds, "Yes, we're philosophizing." Dimmler's appearance on the scene "names" the occasion's tonality. It is "musical," it is "nocturnal" (Mme Rostova asks Dimmler to play a nocturne by Field and as he plays dusk falls, and the silver rays of the moon shine into the sitting room), and, above all, it is "German." It was the Germans who had most exalted music as the expressive language of the soul, in Herder's words "a wonder-music of all the affections, a new magical language of the feelings." The references create a sense of period, reminding Russian readers of the time when their forefathers loved Field, dabbled in German sentimentalism, and read Herder, Schlegel, and Mme. de Staël's *De l'Allemagne*. But Tolstoy does not belong to the interior decorator school of novelists, and he means to do more than furnish his scene with the appropriate accessories. Dimmler's appearance ratifies, as it were, the plunge into Platonic thought that the young people's conversation is about to take.

The key ideas of the Platonic doctrine of memory are introduced into the dialogue by Natasha, whose language now becomes more than simple— it is infantile: "You know, I think . . . that when you remember like that, you remember, remember everything, you remember all the way back to what was earlier, before you were on the earth." The essential seriousness of these ideas propounded in a kind of baby talk is made clear by the sudden interest that Dimmler takes in the conversation. "He had approached the young people with a gentle, condescending smile, but now he spoke as quietly and seriously as they." To understand what in Natasha's naive formulation could interest the philosophical Dimmler, we shall have to translate her ideas back into the language of high philosophy, where they have their origins.

That we "remember" things in our current existence because we knew them in past existences is the very soul of Platonic doctrine. In the *Meno,* Socrates points to memory to answer the question, How can we seek for what we are totally ignorant of? As Alexandre Koyré [in *Discovering Plato*] has put it, "Socrates answers the objection by evoking a myth and invoking a fact. The myth of the pre-existence of souls permits us to conceive of knowledge as a reminiscence, and the fact that it is possible to teach a science to someone ignorant of it without actually 'teaching' him, but on the contrary having him discover it for himself, demonstrates that knowledge is actually merely remembering." In other words, "recollection brings back to our minds knowledge that our soul has always possessed in its own right." The doctrine of recollection originates, then, not in the necessity to affirm the immortality of the soul, but as a means for accounting for our ability to know. It figures in the colloquy between Natasha and Nikolai in its extended form, as it was developed by Socrates in the *Phaedo*. As he waits to drink the hemlock, Socrates is concerned to reassure his disciples that his death is not an occasion for mourning. He does so by affirming the continuity of earthly existence with the true reality, the eternal forms. The philosopher of all men should be happiest to die for he has in this earthly existence beheld the Ideas and he can hope to ascend into that realm "where the god resides in order to be divine"—that is, into the realm of pure forms. It is this continuity of the earthly with the divine that Socrates means when he uses the famous phrase, so critical for Tolstoy's own metaphysics, "Death is an awakening."

This body of ideas is the stuff of Natasha's discourse on remembering. The doctrine of recollection is restated in her simple language as, "You remember all the way back to what was earlier, before you were on the earth." Our apprehension of the realm of pure forms through past existence is adumbrated in her childish metaphysics as, "We are angels there some place, and were here, and from that remember everything." And the continuity of the self in immortality is restated as, "Why do I know what I was before? . . . After all the soul is immortal. It must be so if I will always live as I lived in the past, as I lived for a whole eternity."

I mean to argue that the Platonic doctrine of remembering underlies the shape that *War and Peace* took as a novel, but first it would be well to say something about Tolstoy as a thinker. Tolstoy's contemporaries thought him intellectually muddled, though they admired his gifts as an artist. Tolstoy was for the most part a self-taught man, with both the fresh response and the lack of system that that implies. He had a tremendous appetite for ideas and read voraciously in philosopohy from Plato to Schopenhauer; yet no one would claim that he is a rigorous thinker. Two of the best critics of Tolstoy's work, Boris Eikhenbaum and Viktor Shklovsky, once quarreled about Tolstoy's merits as a thinker. In his major study *Lev Tolstoy* Eikhenbaum had argued that Tolstoy was considerably influenced by the thought of his day. Shklovsky, in keeping with his predilection for popular culture as the source of new art, argued that Tolstoy had been a man of the middle level of cultural life, not really able to follow the philosophical discussions that had so shaped the intellectual life of the 1860s. Both Eikhenbaum and Shklovsky intuited something fundamental to a full description of Tolstoy as thinker. His reading in philosophy and his immersion in the climate of ideas are among the most important experiences that shape

Tolstoy's art. Yet Shklovsky is right to think that there is something peculiar about Tolstoy's relationship to ideas.

Tolstoy as thinker comes into focus only when we understand that he does not belong primarily to the logicians or the analysts among the philosophers. Rather, he belongs to the line of the philosopher-fantasts of whom his idol Rousseau is the prominent example. The philosopher-fantasts are characterized by their resort to revery as well as to logical procedure. Their philosophy is colored by the making of myths and narratives, by the exercise of the literary imagination. Plato was himself a philosopher-fantast and his resort to myths has created a problem for rationalists, who continually find it necessary to reinterpret the Platonic myths into a rationalist framework. The philosopher-fantasts often have an impact more far-reaching and lasting than the philosopher-analysts. Rousseau's work, with its reveries, novel, autobiography, had an impact on the nineteenth century that can hardly be measured. Its influence persists to our day. Tolstoy, like Rousseau, had a generous conception of what philosophy encompassed, and like Rousseau he mingled his philosophizing with fantasizing. Thinking and the creating of narratives were implied in the same gesture of the mind.

Certain interests have made philosophical thinkers find revery a congenial form of mental activity. In particular, problems that have seemed resistant to the application of logic, like the nature of our existence in time, the possibility of immortality, and the content of consciousnes, have led naturally to mythmaking. Revery and myth have been the philosophers' instruments for projection of possible better worlds. Perception, time, and memory have been the great questions for the philosopher-fantasts, and it is not surprising that critics are beginning to find Rousseau and Tolstoy close to Proust.

The question remains, Why has Tolstoy chosen to make Natasha the advocate for Platonic doctrine? The answer lies in Tolstoy's acquaintance with several significant deviations from the doctrine incorporated into the tradition in later times. Tolstoy knew the *Phaedo* directly, but Rousseau and the German romantics had reinforced his predisposition to idealism in the Platonic vein. The very passages we are looking at echo a scene in Goethe's *The Sorrows of Young Werther,* a book that Tolstoy had read a number of times in his youth and reacted to ecstatically. Werther, who is falling into despair over his love for Lotte, who is engaged to the estimable Albert, has been invited by the couple to join them in Lotte's garden at sunset. Lotte and Albert come out as the moon rises, and the three friends make their way to a favorite spot, where "the path is darkened by the adjoining shrubbery, until all ends in an enclosure that has a mysterious aura of loneliness." Moved by the beauty of the moonlight, Lotte says, "I never walk in the moonlight, never, without being reminded of my dead. In the moonlight, I am always filled with a sense of death and of the hereafter. We live on . . . but, Werther, do we meet again? Shall we recognize each other? What do you feel? What do you believe?" Werther responds, "Lotte, we shall meet again. Here and there . . . we shall meet again." Lotte is drawn to tell the story of her young mother, who on her deathbed entrusted her very young children to her care. Lotte has taken their care as a sacred trust. " 'And she had to die in the prime of life,' Lotte continued, 'when her youngest son was not yet six months old. She was not ill for long. She was so calm, so resigned. Only when she saw her children did she feel pain, especially the baby.' " This scene could not have failed to move Tolstoy, whose mother died when he was not yet two. Maria Tolstoy's memory was preserved at Yasnaya Polyana on the same exalted note as Lotte's mother's at Walheim. But what concerns us here is the similar constellation of narrative motifs and philosophical questions. In a nocturnal setting a young woman, speaking simply and without reserve, does not hesitate to raise questions about the immortality of the soul that more sophisticated spirits shy away from. (Indeed, Albert gently tries to dissuade her from the topic.) It would seem that Tolstoy, without necessarily consciously imitating Goethe, is drawing upon types that are deeply embedded in his memory.

A more conscious use of his predecessors occurs in Tolstoy's incorporation of Herder's ideas into the colloquy between Natasha and Nikolai. While working on *War and Peace* and reading the periodicals of the early part of the century for background, Tolstoy had come across an exposition of Herder's ideas which renewed his interest in the Platonic doctrine of recollection. The Herderian text penetrates the drafts of *War and Peace* more deeply than it does the final form of the novel, where it figures in three episodes: the one in which Prince Andrei overhears Tushin discussing the immortality of the soul, the scene on the raft in which Pierre attempts to educate Andrei in what Andrei calls his "Herderian ideas," and the scene we are now examining.

In the drafts and in the text of the novel Tolstoy returns repeatedly to Herder's restatement of the idea that memory is the guarantor of immortality and particularly to the phrase reiterated from Plato, "Death is an awakening." But one article of Herder's version struck Tolstoy as comic. Herder, with his strong biological interests, had tried to give a new turn to the idea of immortality by proposing that we have a specifically biological immortality based on the food chain: each kind devours the beings lower than itself and thereby insures them a continuing immortality in the process of life: "An elephant is the grave of a thousand worms." Though Tolstoy was attracted to the idea of the ladder of beings, in the long run it aroused his scepticism and he finally has his character reject it. The sticking point comes when we try to transfer the neat economy of consumption from those beings lower than us on the ladder to those who might be higher than us: "I don't agree that some kind of higher beings eat us, no." In the exchange between Natasha and Sonya in the music room at Otradnoe, Sonya incorrectly identifies Natasha's belief that one can "remember what happened before one was in the world," as "metempsychosis," and defines it thus: "The Egyptians believed that our souls have lived in animals, and will go back into animals again." Tolstoy is careful to repudiate this deviation and returns to the more purely Platonic doctrine of our continuity with beings higher than ourselves: " 'No, I don't believe we ever were in animals,' said Natasha, still in a whisper though the music had ceased. 'But I am certain that we were angels somewhere *there*, and have been here, and that is why we remember.' "

If Tolstoy rejected the "biological" deviation from Platonic thought, he was more sympathetic to another refinement. Plato had assumed that recollection is a function of the mature man—indeed, it is the function that defines the philosopher. Proclus had changed the locus of our tie with the higher reality by proposing that the child brings into the world visions of an earlier ideal existence which become dimmed by the experiences of earth. Proclus's reinterpretation, filtered into Romantic thought through the Cambridge Platonists, caught writers' imaginations and became a staple of Romantic metaphysics. We are familiar with this doctrine through Wordsworth's "Ode: Intimations of Immortality":

> Our birth is but a sleep and a forgetting:
>   The Soul that rises with us, our life's Star,
>   Hath had elsewhere its setting,
>   And cometh from afar:
>   Not in entire forgetfulness,
>   And not in utter nakedness,
>   But trailing clouds of glory do we come
>   From God, who is our home.

Tolstoy did not have a Coleridge to educate him in Neoplatonic thought, but Karamzin and the *lyubomudry* ("wisdom-lovers") had publicized similar ideas in Russia. The doctrine of preexistence had so many conduits through Romantic thought that a writer so susceptible to the rhetoric of sentimentalism as Tolstoy could hardly have escaped knowing it. Proclus's doctrine was ready to hand to bolster the new emphasis on growth and process as the primary principle of being with its attendant emphasis on the child. That philosophical program is everywhere in Tolstoy, determining the shape of his first book, aptly named *Childhood (Detstvo)*, influencing his theories of pedagogy, and shaping the characters of *War and Peace*.

When Natasha speaks in her infantile language of remembering the world where we were angels before, she represents Proclus's doctrine not only in what she says, but in her person. She is that very child who has come not in entire forgetfulness. The events that she and Nikolai recall from their childhoods have an aura both trivial and fantastical.

> "And do you remember how we rolled hard-boiled eggs in the ballroom and suddenly two old women began spinning round on the carpet? Was that real or not? Do you remember what fun it was?"
>
> "Yes, and do you remember how Papa in his blue overcoat fired a gun in the porch?"

Tolstoy means to affirm that children have a particular power of seizing and remembering the plastic reality of the moment and that the capacity for remembering is a sign of the expressive capacity of the self. Flat Sonya cannot recall much and what she does recall does not awake the poetic feeling experienced by Nikolai and Natasha. The poetry of youthful memories is what Tolstoy means to evoke: "So they went through their memories, smiling with pleasure: not the sad memories of old age, but poetic, youthful ones—those impressions of one's most distant past in which dreams and realities blend—and they laughed with quiet enjoyment." Childhood's poetry naturally carries over into the metaphysical realm, and so, though the rational Dimmler finds eternity hard to comprehend, Natasha explains it with ease: "Why is it difficult to imagine eternity . . . ? It will be now, it will be tomorrow, it will be always, and it was yesterday and the day before yesterday." Natasha's closeness to the undifferentiated state of nature confers on her the authority to speak about immortality and eternity.

What have we discovered by tracing the roots of Natasha's discourse in the Platonic tradition of thought? If we are merely to name these ideas as Platonic, merely to specify an influence, we have not come very far. Platonism is important for *War and Peace* because it provides Tolstoy with an ideational grid that governs his many choices as novelist in constructing the book. We can see the process at work by turning our attention to the families. Tolstoy conceives not only a wide range of principal characters, each with a carefully delineated core of traits, but also family characters, conceptually unified groups which hold individual characters together within their bounds. Each family has a distinct role to play in the work's moral economy; the Rostovs and Bolkonskys represent alternative versions of the good, the "just" life for Tolstoy, just as the Kuragin—Karagin complex (the near-identity of names is revealing) represents the corrupt life of society.

The key to the Rostovs' place in the novel's scheme lies in the very section we are examining. Volume 2, part 4 of *War and Peace* (book 7 in the Maude translation) is devoted to a picture of Rostov family life at the country estate of Otradnoe. It encompasses the scenes of the wolf hunt, the feasting and dancing in the Russian folk style at the uncle's, and the masking party at Shrovetide with its magical sleighride. As life at Otradnoe unfolds, we are treated to the spectacle of vigorous youth indulging in innocent pleasures, but all within a framework of unity of the generations and of the classes. Old Count Rostov is in harmony with his son Nikolai; the hunting master Daniel is accorded full authority within his own sphere, though he is a serf; the masters and serfs join together in the traditional amusements. This section of the novel is unique in its unity and self-containment (to such an extent that it is the part omitted in "abridged" versions of the novel).

This family idyll is one of the most congenial chords in Tolstoy's imagination. How he dreamed upon the theme of Yasnaya is revealed in a remarkable letter he wrote from the Caucasus in 1852 to his Aunt Tatiana:

> Here is how I imagine the happiness that awaits me in the future. The years pass and I find myself, already no longer young, but not yet old, at Yasnaya. My affairs are in order; I have no worries or problems. You are still living at Yasnaya. You have grown a little older, but you are still active and in good health. Life goes on as before: I work in the morning, but we are together almost all day. After dinner in the evening I read something aloud to you that you won't be bored listening to. Then conversation begins. I tell you about my life in the Caucasus, you recount your recollections of the past, of my father and mother. You tell me the horror tales that we used to listen to with frightened eyes and open mouths. We recall those who were

dear to us and are no longer living. You cry and I do, too, but with reconciled tears. We talk of my brothers who come to visit us and of dear Mashenka (Tolstoy's sister), who will visit her beloved Yasnaya with the children for several months every year. We will have no acquaintances. No one will come to bother us and spread gossip. A beautiful dream, but I allow myself to dream of even more. I am married. My wife is gentle, kind and loving and she loves you as I do. Our children call you "grand-mother." You live upstairs in the big house, in that room where grandmother used to live. Everything in the house is the way it was when papa was alive, and we continue to live that life, only changing roles: you will take on the role of grandmother, I the role of papa, though I don't hope ever to deserve it, my wife, that of mama, our children, our role. Mashenka will be in the role of both the aunts, but not unhappy as they were. Even Gasha (Toinette's servant) will be in the place of Praskovia Isaevna (the former housekeeper). The only thing missing is a person who could replace you in a relationship to the whole family. We won't find such a wonderful loving soul. No, you will not have a replacement. . . . If you made me the Russian emperor, if you offered me Peru, in a word if a fairy godmother appeared with a magic wand and asked me what I want, I can say in all honesty with hand on heart: Just one thing, to realize my dream.

When he turned to the writing of *War and Peace* and thought to embody the lives of his forefathers in the narrative, the idyll that he had conceived in youth gave him the stylistic key.

Yet the Otradnoe scenes are not entirely idyllic. They are colored by foreboding. The dark and the light are folded into each other like a marble cake, and Tolstoy keeps before us not only the special joys of country life, but the impending war, the dissolution of the family's way of life due to the father's mismanagement, the going awry of Natasha's marriage to Andrei, and the mother's despair over her children's choice of mates. The section ends, "In the Rostov home it was not merry."

Natasha's colloquy with Nikolai in the sitting room about memory and immortality has all the beauty of "natural" philosophy arising out of the direct experience of untutored and unspoiled souls. Yet she has fallen into revery as a comfort against the dissatisfaction she feels over Andrei's continued absence and the postponement of their marriage. At the end of the conversation she is asked to sing and does so with feeling, but breaks off in a torrent of unexplained weeping. Nor can the Rostov idyll in the country be long sustained. In the next section the family goes to Moscow, where Natasha will be exposed to the very different amusements of society: shopping for her trousseau, the opera, the reading of Mlle George, and the admiration of Anatoli Kuragin. The two sections clearly compose a counterpoint in the novel's structure.

In the Otradnoe scenes both Tolstoy's analytical and compensatory imaginations are at work. He affirms the value of a self-expression rooted in the moral consciousness and connected to a transcendental reality. (Indeed, Tolstoy never loses faith in this most basic of his beliefs. In *What Is Art?* [*Chto takoe iskusstvo?*], written toward the end of his life, we find him still struggling to hold self-expression together with moral purpose as natural and reconcilable parts of a true aesthetics.) While his compensatory imagination creates the idyll in which the values can be made manifest, his analytical imagination shows how reality departs from them. Otradnoe is the flawed earthly paradise that nevertheless links us to the true world of innocence and truth, which in Plato's view is retained dimly in our memories and seized again by philosophy, or in the romantic view remains accessible to the innocent consciousness.

Why are the Rostovs the proper inhabitants of the idyllic world of Otradnoe? We shall have to turn once again to the function of memory in the philosophical and literary tradition. When Socrates was confronted with the necessity of showing the continuity between the world of ordinary human perception and the world of the ideal forms, it was to memory that he turned as the guarantor of their joining. But the doctrine of recollection also had implications for the individual self's unity. As the memory reaches backward to recover our knowledge of the higher truth, it also reaches toward the future, toward what we ideally will become. Memory becomes the chief instrument for achieving the unity of consciousness over time, with all the moral resonance that Platonic doctrine gives to that unity. The doctrine of recollection gives a cue to the novelist, whose need for a coherent sense of character, a theory of human action, and a ground of motivation is satisfied by its provisions.

Rousseau was the first of the modern novelists to understand the significance of memory and to test its possibilities. His preoccupation with individual psychology made him acutely aware of the intermittences of character:

> Everything upon earth is in continuous flux. Nothing in it retains
> a form that is constant and fixed, and our affections, attached

to eternal things, necessarily pass and change like the things themselves. Always, ahead of or behind us, they recall the past which no longer exists, or they anticipate a future which often will never come to pass: there is nothing there solid enough for the heart to attach itself to.

The viable self is called into doubt by the flux of experience, raising the question, Is memory powerful enough to withstand the "I's" disparate and contradictory movements? The individual's problem of finding an autonomous self becomes the author's problem. Not only must the author find ways of achieving whole characters in the face of doubt about the unity of the self, he must also overcome the disintegrating effect of the lacunae in the character's experiences which the selectivity of narrative makes inevitable. His task is doubled.

La Nouvelle Héloïse is one of the most complicated novels ever written on the powers of recollection and retrospection. Rousseau realizes the potentiality of the epistolary form to make even experience that is immediately past subject to the organizing and unifying powers of recall. In their letters Julie, St. Preux, and Claire mirror back and forth to each other a finite set of experiences, made infinitely rich by multiple reflection. Not only is recollection the implicit organizing principle of the novel's structure, but Rousseau more directly confronts the problem of memory in the novel's exposition. After the lovers have been separated, Julie affirms to St. Preux the power of memory to overcome the fundamental changes that occur in the self through time: "As long as those pure and delightful moments return to the memory, it is not possible that thou shouldst cease to love what renders them sweet to thee, that the enchantment of moral beauty shouldst ever be affaced from thy mind." But after Julie has renounced St. Preux to marry the husband chosen by her parents, her faith is called into question. Her wise husband applies what has come to be known as "M. de Wolmar's method" to convince St. Preux that his feeling for Julie is a relic of the past and has no validity in the present.

> It is not Julie de Wolmar with whom he is in love, it is Julie d'Étange. . . . The wife of another is not his mistress; the mother of two children is no longer his former pupil. It is true that she resembles her greatly, and that she often recalls to him the memory of her. He loves her in time past.

M. de Wolmar takes a risky step to test his theory: he invites St. Preux to become the tutor of his children, and he demonstrates his certainty in the outcome by going away and leaving the former lovers tête-à-tête. And indeed his "cure" works. St. Preux acknowledges that the Julie he loved was the Julie of memory and not the "real" Julie of the present. In allowing this outcome, Rousseau establishes the fluid view of character tht will dominate romantic literature and persist into realism. Yet if M. de Wolmar successfully proves the power of time over St. Preux's love, he is disproven in the end by Julie's constancy, for Julie confesses on her deathbed that love for St. Preux has persisted in her memory against all attempts to eradicate it. She thus has the power to reconstitute the past in the present and restore the self to wholeness.

Like so much of Rousseau's text, the lesson that memory is the key to the self's wholeness sank deep into Tolstoy's consciousness. Memory not only gives coherence to the characters of Nikolai and Natasha, who are depicted as having a rich shared experience extending far beyond what can actually be conveyed in the novel, it is the key to the Rostovs' unity as a family group. Here Tolstoy returns to his incipient Platonism, envisioning the Rostovs as the novel's link with the remembered past, including, as Natasha's colloquy shows, the past that exists before birth. Nikolai and Natasha's shared memories push us back to the boundary between the earthly life and the realm from which we come (perhaps) trailing clouds of glory. The tie to childhood memory marks the Rostovs' way of being in the world and the life choices they make.

If the Rostovs pick up the thread of life as it flows out of the source, the Bolkonskys are connected to the continuum at its other end, where in death it rejoins eternity. In Prince Nikolai Bolkonsky we see the present disappearing into the maw of history as one generation gives way to another. Upon the approach of death, Prince Nikolai thinks back to his youth at the court of Catherine the Great, recalls his rivalry with the favorite, Potyomkin, and remembers his struggle with Zubov over her coffin about his right to kiss her hand. He occupies himself with composing his memoirs, which are to be given to the emperor upon his death. His recollections lead him to think, "Oh, quicker, quicker! To get back to that time and have done with all the present! Quicker, quicker—and if only they would leave me in peace!" Recollection makes time whole for him, not by joining him to the eternal world of forms, but by reuniting him with the events that gave meaning to his life as a public man. Of all the public men in the novel, only Kutuzov has a claim to greater dignity of person or clearer rectitude in the public sphere. Nevertheless, in Prince Bolkonsky Tolstoy shows us the limitations of even the best public man.

Andrei and Maria, while resembling their father in high-minded devotion to duty, express themselves in modes more charcteristic of Tolstoy's

Platonism. Andrei comes to be the center of Tolstoy's meditations upon the fluid boundary between life and death. In 1865, when the opening sections of *War and Peace* were just appearing, under the title *1805,* Tolstoy wrote playfully, yet revealingly, to his cousin, who had inquired about Prince Andrei's prototype:

> In the Battle of Austerlitz which is yet to be described, but with which I began the novel, I needed a brilliant young man to die; in the further course of the novel I only needed old Bolkonsky and his daughter; but since it is awkward to write about a character not connected with anything in the novel, I decided to make the brilliant young man the son of old Bolkonsky. Then he came to interest me, a role was found for him in the further course of the novel, and I took pity on him, only wounding him severely instead of letting him die.

"Brilliant" (*blestyashchy*) is in many ways the key to Andrei's character. In the context of the era it means first of all socially brilliant—belonging to the aristocratic society and acting there with perfect comme il faut. Prince Andrei is in fact a persuasive image of aristocratic hauteur and noblesse oblige. He represents the aristocratic ideal in its substantial form in contrast, say, to Hippolyte Kuragin, a fool posing as an arbiter of society, or Boris Drubetskoi, a phoney and an *arriviste.* But Tolstoy does not mean to assert a St. Simonian sense of grandeur: his elevation of Andrei is in the mode of the metaphysical dandy, whose social impeccability becomes the outward sign of his inner spiritual grace. In Russian as in English "brilliant" points finally to the scintillation that makes the hero the "shining one." It prepares us for Andrei's turn to the light.

It is not surprising, then, that Tolstoy's merciful reprieve turns out to be temporary. Perhaps the most critical moment for the development of the novel came late in its writing, when Tolstoy discovered that indeed he was going to let Prince Andrei die. A sizeable portion of the novel had been set in type. Tolstoy was working on the concluding parts within the framework of his original design: all the principal characters would survive. Prince Andrei would be reconciled with Natasha, who would nurse him during his convalescence from the wound incurred at Borodino, but upon learning of Pierre's love for her, he would step aside in favor of his friend. His abdication would prepare the denouement that Tolstoy had intended from the start: Pierre would wed Natasha, Nikolai—Maria. The heroes would be reunited at Kutuzov's farewell to the troops. Indeed, "all's well that ends well," as Tolstoy had it in his projected title.

Still, Andrei's stepping aside was a weak move in the plot, and Tolstoy returned to it to find a more plausible solution. The solution rose to him out of the web of connections already preexisting in his understanding of Andrei as a character: Prince Andrei would die. No scene in *War and Peace* more "stands for" the novel in the reader's consciousness than that of Prince Andrei's delirium in the hut at Mytishchi with its celebrated images of the "hovering fly" and the "edifice of needles" that rises and falls above his face. And yet the manuscript was ready for the printer and no such passages were there. In the first version, Natasha, wearing her nightdress, came to Andrei's bedside to ask his forgiveness. In his softened state he forgave her, as he had forgiven Anatole in the hospital tent. The scene bore the ethical message of Christian love but lacked metaphysical dimension.

The decision to resolve the problem of plot by having Andrei die set in motion a tremulous structure of associations connecting the concept of memory to death and immortality. Since memory is not only the power of recall, but also the link between reality and the higher world, it is the philosopher's instrument in the quest to reach the ideal forms. So thought Plato. Using the Platonic doctrine as his key, Tolstoy now returned to the printer's copy of the manuscript and added the passages describing Andrei's delirium in its margins. He followed through with the scenes at Yaroslavl where Andrei engages in "the last spiritual struggle between life and death, in which death gained the victory." He wrote with such sureness of purpose that the scenes were published in their first versions almost without corrections.

Prince Andrei's visions as he approaches death return the novel decisively to its Platonic core: death is an awakening in which the philosopher's lofty search for truth will be rewarded by his becoming one with the eternal ideas. Seen in this light much in Andrei's character becomes newly intelligible to us. His austerity can be seen as an intimation of that philosophical asceticism that Socrates enjoins upon those who would seek truth. His estrangement from earthly life, which frightened the life-loving Rostovs when Natasha became engaged to him, intensifies in his last days:

> He was conscious of an aloofness from everything earthly and a strange and joyous lightness of existence. Without haste or agitation he awaited what was coming. That inexorable, eternal, distant, and unknown—the presence of which he had felt continually all his life—was now near to him and, by the strange lightness he experienced, almost comprehensible and palpable.

It is significant that childhood memory is almost totally suppressed in the Bolkonskys in spite of their strong family feeling. The one moment of shared memory between Maria and Andrei is mentioned to negate it: "[Maria] smiled, pronouncing the word 'Andryusha.' Clearly, she herself found it strange to think that this severe, handsome man was that same Andryusha, the thin, mischievous boy, the companion of her childhood." The Bolkonskys put childhood behind them to advance toward the reality of the pure forms. Theirs is the forward projection of consciousness—not memory but vision. They turn from watching the shadows on the wall and look into the light.

Socrates has set out with complete clarity the conditions for knowing the pure reality:

> [I]f ever we are going to obtain pure knowledge, we must get away from the body, and with the soul itself see things themselves. And then it would seem, we shall have that which we desire, that which we say we are in love with, wisdom; we shall have it when we are departed, so signifies the argument, and not while we are living; for it is impossible to have pure knowledge of anything whatsoever with the body present, there are two alternatives. Either we never can attain to knowledge, or we can attain it only after death; for then the soul will be alone and by itself, without the body, and before that it will not. . . . [A]nd thus, pure, emancipated from the unreason of the body, it is probable we shall join with beings of like nature, and through ourselves know all the pure reality.

Andrei's getting of wisdom is unfolded for us on three planes. First, the physical process of his disease leads to the weakening of the body's hold on the mind and frees it to seek the true reality. Then the philosophical process through which the mind reaches into the unknown and retrieves reality is adumbrated on a series of aphoristic passages. The physical and mental processes connect with each other in the delirium of Andrei's fever, which is the body's decay but the mind's freedom. Tolstoy makes his most brilliant narrative move on a third level by finding a metaphor appropriate to the exalted nature of the theme: an objective correlative for the pure reality. Socrates' notion of the other reality seems to be that of a convocation of philosophers. Herder sees it mirroring the biological variety of living things. Tolstoy reaches for a metaphor that will convey the otherness that must be native to a reality separated from our own. "Together with the sound of this whispering music, Prince Andrei felt, that over his face, over its very center, there was rising some kind of strange airy structure of thin needles or splinters." The structure of shining rays (*luchina* means a splinter of wood used for light like a candle) is a pulsating structure of truth, the

Platonic Idea itself, as yet undifferentiated into its verbal axioms by the process of analysis. Here we need to be reminded once again that memory in the Platonic tradition is something more than recall of the past; it is the function of mind that connects us to the higher reality. In the Mytishchi scene memory as such does not figure, but the threads leading from the doctrine of recollection bind the scene together and furnish forth the truths Andrei arrives at in the weeks before his death. Vinogradov long ago remarked the aphoristic quality of Andrei's thoughts, exemplified in this characteristic passage: "Love hinders death. Love is life. All, everything that I understand, I understand only because I love. Everything is united by it alone. Love is God, and to die means that I, a particle of love shall return to the general and eternal source." There are verbal crystallizations of bits of the truth condensed out of the seamless perfection of Truth itself. The phrases' laconism reflects that fragmentation, as it reflects truth's weightiness.

It is undoubtedly no accident that when Tolstoy sought a place in his novel for "a brilliant young man who was to die," he attached him to that narrative core devoted to evoking the sainted memory of his dead mother. Princess Maria provides the key to the Bolkonsky family's definition as "those who will die." Though she does not herself die in the course of the narrative, her early death is predicted in the epilogue. The death of his mother was what was given to Tolstoy as fact. What required invigoration by the powers of imagination was the story of her life. But the life must be one in which the meaning of her death is prefigured. A passage late in the novel directs us to the right understanding.

> As suddenly when the internal light is lit there shows forth on the sides of a carved and painted lantern with unexpectedly strik-ing beauty that intricate, skillful, artistic work that had earlier seemed coarse, dark, and senseless, so Princess Maria's face sud-denly was transformed. For the first time all that pure spiritual travail through which she had lived up to now appeared on the surface. All her inward labor, that labor of her own self-dissat-isfaction, her suffering, her yearning towards the good, her hu-mility, love and self-sacrifice—all that shone now in these radiant eyes, in the delicate smile, in every feature of her tender face.

The comparison of Maria's face to a magic lantern continues the pattern of metaphysical reference that has been worked out in earlier passages of the novel. The imagery links Maria to Andrei's heroic spiritual travail. Tolstoy had introduced the magic lantern into Prince Andrei's vision on the eve of

Borodino: "All life appeared to him like magic-lantern pictures at which he had long been gazing by artificial light through a glass. Now he suddenly saw those sadly daubed pictures in clear daylight and without a glass." For Andrei the lantern is an image of the false world of appearances, akin to the flickering shadows on the wall of Plato's cave, and it prepares the way for the renunciation of earthly reality Andrei will achieve on his deathbed. For Maria the perspective has been turned: instead of looking outward to the false pictures cast by the flickering flame, we look inward to the source of light. Maria is thus included among that elect group of characters— Natasha, Andrei, Pierre—to whom Tolstoy vouchsafes visionary experience. She "sees through" to something beyond the world of appearances and even to another life. But it is Maria's destiny as Tolstoy has created her to represent holiness in the lowly way—through the example of her humility and Christian charity. Hers is the holiness of the ethical life based on piety rather than of the questing mystical spirit.

The doctrine of memory serves, then, the compensatory side of Tolstoy's imagination. He holds in his mind the idyll that reality must be judged by. Once it has been called into question, there is need to discover a new equilibrium on which a just universal moral economy can be founded. That desire to compensate, to find a new just equilibrium in which the essential rightness of life will be confirmed, is a powerful stimulus to the writing of *War and Peace*. Tolstoy originally meant to call the novel *All's Well That Ends Well,* and the epilogue brings us to that happy ending in which the right pairs are joined in fruitful unions leading to the continuation of the best potentialities of life. But a confirmation of life resting on a partial view, one excluding the harsher aspects of reality, would be trivial. Tolstoy includes all the evils which prevent us from attaining the ideal forms in this human life: moral corruption, desires of the flesh, cruelty, war, death. Every kind of degradation, every kind of threat, must be overcome if true equilibrium is to be achieved. If we compare *War and Peace* to *Anna Karenina,* we see at once how strong the compensatory imagination is in the first, where anything, even death, can be transformed into a vehicle of happiness or enlightenment. In *Anna Karenina,* on the contrary, reality has infinite capacity to harm. The doctrine of memory is the foundation of the just equilibrium striven for and achieved in *War and Peace*.

Forms of Life and Death: *War and Peace*

Martin Price

Nicholas Rostov moves from the inside of one form of life to the inside of another when, after informing his father of his enormous gambling debt, he returns to the regiment. There, "bound in one narrow, unchanging frame, he experienced the same sense of peace, of moral support, and the same sense of being at home here in his own place, as he had felt under the parental roof. But here was none of all that turmoil of the world at large." He is free of difficult choices and awkward explanations; one had only to do "what was clearly, distinctly, and definitely ordered." (This is very much the appeal of military life for Vronsky as well.)

It is not, however, so simple as Nicholas might wish. He is troubled when the emperor fails to grant his petition on Denisov's behalf. Nicholas is even more profoundly troubled by the mutual esteem the emperor and Napoleon display at the Peace of Tilsit. Nicholas doesn't know quite what disturbs him, and the disturbance takes the form of vivid memories rather than reflection, memories he has repressed in his state of hopefulness:

> Terrible doubts arose in his soul. Now he remembered Denisov with his changed expression . . . and the whole hospital, with arms and legs torn off and its dirt and disease. So vividly did he recall that hospital stench of dead flesh that he looked around to see where the smell came from. Next he thought of that self-satisfied Bonaparte, with his small white hand, who was now

From *Forms of Life: Character and Moral Imagination in the Novel.* © 1983 by Yale University. Yale University Press, 1983.

> an Emperor, liked and respected by Alexander. Then why those
> severed arms and legs and those dead men? . . . He caught him-
> self harboring such strange thoughts that he was frightened.

Rather than allow himself to acknowledge such thoughts, Nicholas drinks
heavily and rebukes a fellow officer who expresses the thoughts that trouble
Nicholas himself. The officer provides him with an occasion to fight down
his doubts. How can you judge the Emperor's actions! While the fellow
officer protests that he has never criticized the emperor, Nicholas continues:
"If once we begin judging and arguing about everything, nothing sacred
will be left! That way we shall be saying there is no God—nothing!"
Nicholas comes in from the frontiers of disbelief; he has been made all too
much aware of the medium, of the assumptions and presuppositions he is
terrified of losing; and he regains assurance with a mixture of wine and
rationalization.

Nicholas's mother, the Countess Rostov, provides us with a good
instance of someone who has moved outside the life she has always lived.
She has lost her young son Petya and her husband:

> She ate, drank, slept, or kept awake, but did not *live*. Life gave
> her no new impressions. She wanted nothing from life but tran-
> quillity, and that tranquillity only death could give her. But until
> death came she had to go on living. . . . She talked only because
> she physically needed to exercise her tongue and lungs. . . .
> What for people in their full vigor is an aim was for her . . .
> merely a pretext.
>
> (First Epilogue)

One of the most consistent ways in which Tolstoy treats these forms
of life we take for granted is in his account of military command. The tenor
of his argument throughout is that the plans of commanders have little
relevance to what occurs. There are too many imponderables, there is too
vast a field to encompass. Those like Kutuzov who recognize the nature of
this vast play of forces can at least learn to work with them. When Kutuzov
listened to battle reports, he attended not to the words spoken or the facts
reported, but to "the expression of face and of voice of those who were
reporting." He knew how few sane choices could be made by a commander
and how much depended on "that intangible force called the spirit of the
army." Kutuzov, therefore, listens and watches with a "concentrated quiet
attention," for he recognizes the true framework which it is not customary
to acknowledge. He knows military operations from the inside.

A commander in chief, Tolstoy observes, "is never dealing with the beginning of any event." He is "always in the midst of a series of shifting events and so he never can at any moment consider the whole import of an event that is occurring. Moment by moment the event is imperceptibly shaping itself, and at every moment . . . the commander in chief is in the midst of a most complex play of intrigues, worries, contingencies," etc. The general may give orders so as to make whatever must happen seem to have been brought about by his will, but, Tolstoy insists, the sense of freedom which we have and must act upon should not delude us into thinking we have greater powers than we do. "Only unconscious action bears fruit, and he who plays a part in an historic event never understands its significance. If he tries to realize it his efforts are fruitless. Most events represent the convergence of wills unknown to each other, of circumstances which are never sufficiently recognized. It is only when an event is past that we can see it completely. Just as Kutuzov listens for what the voice rather than the words reveals, so again when he addresses the troops, they do not hear his words, but they understand his "feeling of majestic triumph combined with pity for the foe and consciousness of the justice" of the Russian cause.

We see Kutuzov, then, improvising a series of tactical retreats, allowing the French forces to occupy Moscow, watching them founder in their ill-conceived retreat. He does not play the game of dazzling strategy and glorious victory; only he, in fact, knows that the Battle of Borodino was a victory for the Russians and the turning point in Napoleon's expedition. Kutuzov has his own game, if that is the word for it; he is like the patient defendant who keeps prudently deferring a trial until the plaintiff litigates himself into insolvency. For his game is not winning a lawsuit but defeating the plaintiff; and sapping the plaintiff's will or his fortune is less costly and risky than confronting him in court. This is perhaps an unattractive account of Kutuzov's method, but one must think of him as a defendant who believes so completely in the justness of his cause that he does not need to declare it or defend it in a court.

Kutuzov is a man who exhibits little distinction of manner; he is corpulent and untidy, in some ways resembling both Pierre and Karataev. What he shares with them is an unheroic, even antiheroic, manner. Tolstoy is full of sympathy for the soldier's patriotic feeling, but he tends to celebrate the greatness that is thrust upon men, stability to endure and wit to improvise. There is no better instance than Prince Andrew's snatching up the fallen standard at Austerlitz as Napoleon had done at the Bridge of Arcola, and leading an improbable charge against the French. "Forward, lads! he shouted in a voice as piercing as a child's." The final simile is telling; there is a wonderful naivety about his action, and yet he is followed by a battalion in the face of the cannon which the French have captured and are about to turn around. As Andrew lies wounded on the battlefield, even the standard missing, he hears Napoleon remark of him, "That's a fine death."

Prince Andrew is the antithesis of such unheroic figures as Pierre and Kutuzov. And, like all the Bolkonskis in the novel, he has turned away from life. We first encounter him at Anna Schérer's soirée, where the deadliest sin is to be natural and where Andrew gives the impression of having found everyone, but most of all his wife, "so tiresome that it wearied him to look at or listen to them." Later in private conversation Pierre sees a new aspect of Andrew, a passion of nervous excitement and morbid criticism. Andrew feels himself trapped by marriage, consigned to the role of a court lackey, caught in a narrow circle of gossip, ceremony, and triviality. He is about to go to war as a means of escape.

Throughout the novel we see Andrew looking for something to believe in with heroic devotion and abandon, but always prepared, at the least threat to the perfection of that faith, to withdraw into sardonic disenchantment. There is some part of him that is drawn to the glories of power; he enjoys helping other young men to win the success which his pride cannot accept for himself. He is ready to admire a court official like Speranksi, but equally ready to be disenchanted. There is about Prince Andrew something of the Byronic hero who yearns for a greatness he can trust, but who is always afraid of being taken in and ready to meet every occasion with irony. This is a pride that seems superior, but proves, as the novel unfolds, less robust, less intelligent, than Pierre's often clumsy and childish tenacity. As he lies on the battlefield, Andrew concentrates upon the "lofty sky, not clear yet still immeasurably lofty." Yes, he thinks, "all is vanity, all falsehood, except that infinite sky." This is the peace of abstention, the repose of a mind that cannot be deceived because it has chosen emptiness (or one might call it purity). So, when Napoleon stops over him to admire what he takes to be a hero's corpse, he seems to Andrew "a small, insignificant creature compared with what was passing now between himself and that lofty, infinite sky with the clouds flying over it." It is once again "the lofty, equitable and kindly sky" that makes Napoleon's joy in victory seem nothing but "paltry vanity," a "short-sighted delight at the misery of others." The loss of blood and the apparent nearness of death make Andrew think of "the insignificance of greatness, the unimportance of life . . . and the still greater unimportance of death." How good it would be, he thinks, if "everything were as clear and simple" as it seems to his devout sister, but he cannot pray either to an "incomprehensible God," the "Great All or Nothing," or "to that God who has been sewn into this amulet by Mary." All that is great is incomprehensible, all he can comprehend is unimportant.

I think we can see a pattern here—an intense idealism that demands more certainty than life can afford, a readiness to turn at the least threat of uncertainty to a cynical disdain. Both are forms of withdrawal from the actual, whether impatience to redeem and transfigure it or scorn for its inadequacy and betrayal. We see only the sense of betrayal in his treatment of his wife, and her reproachful face on her deathbed leaves him feeling guilty for having failed to love her. (We do not know why he married her or how he saw or imagined her then.) He can say to Pierre that there are only two evils in life: remorse and illness. "The only good is the absence of those evils." Pierre is not persuaded. "To live only so as not to do evil and not to have to repent is not enough. I lived like that, I lived for myself and ruined my life." His phrase "lived for myself" is a commentary on Andrew's defensiveness, and Andrew accepts it. He has, he says, tried to live for others, in the search for glory; but he has become calmer now that he lives only for himself or for those few people who are, so to speak, extensions of himself, his family.

Pierre is not discouraged by Andrew's mixture of realism and cynicism, and Andrew comes to respond to Pierre's insistent faith with a "radiant, childlike, tender look," as if he could see once more in the "high, everlasting sky" what he had seen as he lay wounded at Austerlitz. It awakens in turn something slumbering in himself, "something that was best within him." He is prepared for a new ideal form of life, which he is about to find in Natasha.

Before he comes to that, he encounters once more the ancient oak on his estate which seems to tell him of the changelessness and futility of life: a "stupid, meaningless, constantly repeated fraud! . . . There is no spring, no sun, no happiness!" And Andrew withdraws from life again into a restful, mournfully pleasant, rather sentimental "hopelessness." It is always at such a moment that a Tolstoyan hero encounters a force of renewed life. When he sees Natasha he wonders, "What is she so glad about? . . . Why is she so happy?" The delight Natasha finds in her life is mysterious to him, and once he overhears her intense response to the beauty of the night, the ancient oak is transfigured. In his own seizure of an "unreasoning springtime feeling of joy and renewal" he is at last ready to give up living for himself alone.

There is a significant intertwining of two series of events, Andrew's attachment to Natasha and his regard for Speranski. He has found in Speranski the ideal of a perfectly rational and virtuous man, and he feels for him an admiration like that he had once felt for Napoleon. But just after the ball at which Natasha dances so radiantly, and where Andrew begins to love her, he finds himself seeing through Speranski's artifices and condescension. All of his hard work on the Legal Code now seems useless and foolish. He turns all the more eagerly to a world of personal feeling. As Natasha sings, Andrew finds himself choked with tears. For what? he wonders, and concludes: "The chief reason was a sudden, vivid sense of the terrible contrast between something infinitely great and illimitable within him" (one thinks of the illimitable, overarching sky) and "that limited and material something that he, and even she, was. This contrast weighed on and yet cheered him while she sang." This reconciliation of the infinite and the immediate becomes an opening up of freedom and responsibility; he believes at last in "the possibility of happiness."

When Andrew learns of Natasha's relation with Anatole and has accepted the breaking of their engagement, we find him defending Speranski, who has fallen from power, against the charges of others. He finds relief from his other grief and anger in argument, and when he learns from Pierre of Natasha's illness, he voices his regret and smiles very much like his father, "coldly, maliciously, and unpleasantly." He has once again withdrawn into a defensive pride and, so to speak, seceded from life.

Prince Andrew, like Nicholas Rostov, loses himself in his regiment; his hatred for his past emerges whenever he meets a former acquaintance. Then he grows "spiteful, ironical, and contemptuous." As he returns to the estate at Bald Hills, he encounters two small peasant girls who have carried plums from the hothouse in their skirts and hide when they see Andrew. He tries to spare their feelings, and for a while they involve him in a shared life: "A new sensation of comfort and relief came over him when, seeing these girls, he realized the existence of other human interests entirely aloof from his own." It is too much to sustain. When he sees the soldiers bathing nearby in a pond, splashing happily and laughing, he feels a sudden disgust with their naked bodies and his own. It is a feeling he does not understand, and it contravenes that moment of involvement he felt in the girls' pleasure. It seems like a withdrawal from everything alive in others and himself, a cruel asceticism which is a sentence upon his own life.

We see that again in the cold white light which seems to descend over all reality upon the eve of the Battle of Borodino. It is a fierce light "without shadow, without perspective, and without distinction of outline." He welcomes it as clear daylight and truth as opposed to the lantern-slide images that have deceived him all his life. (He is outside the forms of life he once accepted, and the figure is close to Wittgenstein's.) All that has claimed him for life now seems "simple, pale, and crude in the cold white light of this morning." He thinks with special bitterness, which is also an unacknowledged yearning, of his romantic belief in Natasha. It is hard to extirpate altogether the sense of himself: he looks at the sunlit row of birches and thinks, "That all this should still be, but no me." And in the process the trees and all the scene about him become "terrible and menacing."

In retrospect one sees Prince Andrew's fluctuations between life and some form of externality—aloofness or detachment or defensiveness—some form, that is, of death. His trust in life is insufficient, in part because he brings to it tyrannical ideals; but even those may be a means of assaying its impossibility so that he may justify his retreat. Some, of course, of Andrew's attitudes are such as Tolstoy held, or had held, or would hold; they were always a part of him and they are given their life here in opposition to the attitudes of Pierre and Natasha, which were no less his own.

If Andrew fluctuates between two forms of life—between withdrawal into asceticism and expansion into incautious love—his father tries to impose the pattern of the life now denied him, in exerting his command upon his plain, unloved, and pious daughter. And Mary, in turn, tries to shape her life after the example of Jesus, in a constant putting of others before her. Some part of Mary fights this continual self-abasement; there is enough force of life in her to demand some fulfillment, however frighteningly the demands present themselves.

Pierre, in contrast to the Bolkonskis, tries ceaselessly to bring himself within the frame of life, enduring humiliation, accepting entrapment. "All this had to be and could not be otherwise," he reflects when the proposal he has not yet quite made is accepted by Hélène's father. "It is good because it's definite and one is rid of the old tormenting doubts." Pierre is often a comic figure, in part because he behaves repetitiously, in part because he is without pride, a man wholly open to what he finds in himself, somewhat like Boswell or Tolstoy himself in his curiosity about his feelings and his powers. He engages in a succession of self-deceptions. He feels, as an initiate into Freemasonry, "that he had been vicious only because he had somehow forgotten how good it is to be virtuous." He soars into visions of his future benevolence, persuaded by his warm feeling that he has already attained moral perfection. Later, his steward stages performances by grateful serfs who shower Pierre with gratitude.

But increasingly, even as he falls repeatedly into illusion, Pierre finds forms of active goodness, as in his reassurance of Natasha at the time of her disgrace, his delicacy in speaking with her during his illness, his participation in the battery's activities at Borodino, his rescue of a child. Even his demented plan to assassinate Napoleon is conceived as rescue and service for his fellow Russians. Natasha accepts his kindness without gratitude: "it seemed so natural for him to be kind to everyone that there was no merit in his kindness."

As a prisoner Pierre sheds the qualities that have made him seem foolish; the experience of captivity is one he assumes, so to speak, for the other characters in the novel. For while Andrew and Natasha undergo great change, Pierre's is the change which most fully combines thought and feeling, and which seems to arise from the deepest engagement with reality. He is freed of tormenting doubts; he has lost that freedom which once made the choice of occupation indissolubly difficult. He is reduced to a life where the very qualities that had made him seem clumsy in society now become appropriate and all but make him seem a hero.

His response to the landscape and the sky about him shows his difference from Prince Andrew. He sees the sun rising, making everything "sparkle in the glad light"—the cupolas and crosses of the convent, the hoarfrost on the grass, the distant hills and the river. Pierre feels "a new joy and strength in life such as he had never known before." It is at night in the brilliance of a full moon that Tolstoy presents one of those sacramental moments that are so essential to his sense of life. Pierre achieves a transcendence which is not a separation or withdrawal like Andrew's but a moment of ecstatic inclusiveness—the bivouacs and campfires, the forests and fields visible in the distance. "And further still, beyond those forests and fields, the bright oscillating limitless distance that lured one to its depths. Pierre glanced up at the sky and the twinkling stars in its faraway depths. 'And all that is me, all that is within me, and it is all I.' " He smiles at the effort men have made to imprison his soul, and then he lies down to sleep "beside his companions."

As Pierre finds freedom in imprisonment and learns what can be endured, he realizes "the full strength of life in man," he gains the power to control his attention and direct his thought. When Karataev is executed Pierre can concentrate his attention upon the French soldiers who have shot him. In another moment of defamiliarization, he recognizes one of them as the man who had burned his shirt while drying it two days before and had aroused laughter among them. At each moment that his mind turns in grief to Karataev, a consoling memory from the past deflects his attention. The inability of the mind to close in upon its suffering seems in one view helpless passivity before its associations, in another a genius for survival.

Chronology

1828	Lev Nikolaevich Tolstoy born August 28 at Yasnaya Polyana, his father's estate, eighty miles from Moscow.
1830	Tolstoy's mother dies.
1837	Tolstoy's father dies.
1841	Upon the death of their guardian, Alexandra Osten-Saken, the Tolstoy children move to Kazan.
1844	Tolstoy enters Kazan University in the Department of Eastern Languages but transfers to the Faculty of Law the following year.
1847	Leaves the University without graduating and returns to Yasnaya Polyana, where he attempts a program of social reform directed at the peasants.
1851	Goes to the Caucasus with his eldest brother Nikolai to serve as a volunteer in the army.
1852–53	Enlists officially in the army. *Childhood* published in the *Contemporary*. During campaigns in the Caucasus, Tolstoy writes *Boyhood* and stories of army life. Outbreak of the Crimean War.
1854	Tolstoy promoted to ensign and transferred to the Crimea. *Boyhood* published in the *Contemporary*.
1855	Writes *Sevastopol Sketches*.
1856	Death of Tolstoy's brother Dmitri. Tolstoy contemplates marrying Valerya Arseneva. Resigns from army and returns to Yasnaya Polyana. *The Two Hussars* published in the *Contemporary*.
1857	Tolstoy visits western Europe. Writes "Lucerne." *Youth* published in the *Contemporary*.
1859	*Family Happiness* and *Three Deaths* published; critical reception is less enthusiastic than for his earlier works. Founds an experimental school for peasant children at Yasnaya Polyana.

1860	Tolstoy leaves for western Europe. Death of his brother Nikolai.
1861	Tolstoy returns to Russia. Publishes *Yasnaya Polyana,* an educational journal. Quarrels with Turgenev, challenging him to a duel. Appointed District Arbiter of the Peace. Resumes school work at Yasnaya Polyana.
1862	Resigns as Arbiter. Marries Sofya Andreevna Bers, daughter of a court physician. Closes Yasnaya Polyana school.
1863	Publishes *The Cossacks.* The first of his thirteen children born.
1864–69	Tolstoy writes and publishes *War and Peace.*
1870–72	Begins a novel about Peter the Great, never finished. Reopens school. While reading Pushkin, he is inspired with an idea for a new novel.
1873–77	Writes *Anna Karenina,* which is serialized in the *Russian Herald.* Despite favorable critical reactions, Tolstoy expresses deep dissatisfaction with the novel and confesses having great trouble writing it. He quarrels with publisher Katkov, who refuses to print the epilogue to the novel because of its political content.
1878	Reconciliation between Tolstoy and Turgenev. Tolstoy's great moral crisis leads him into a period of intense theological study and questioning.
1882	Publishes *Confession;* writes *What I Believe.*
1884	*What I Believe* banned.
1885	Writes stories for Chertkov's *The Intermediary.*
1886	*The Death of Ivan Ilych* published. Tolstoy's play *The Power of Darkness* offends the Tsar, and its performance is forbidden.
1891	*The Kreutzer Sonata* published.
1893–96	*The Kingdom of God Is within You, Christianity and Patriotism, Reason and Religion, Religion and Morality, Master and Man, How to Read the Gospels.*
1898	Publishes *What Is Art?*
1899	Publishes *Resurrection,* which he has been writing for ten years.
1901	Excommunicated by the Holy Synod of the Russian Orthodox Church. *Reply to the Synod's Edict.*
1904–5	Finishes *Hadji Murad.* Writes *Alyosha the Pot* and *The Posthumous Notes of Fyodor Kuzmich.* Beginning of Russo-Japanese War and the 1905 Revolution.

1908–9   Finishes *I Cannot Be Silent!*, a protest against the hanging of the 1905 revolutionaries. Growing quarrels between Tolstoy and his wife.

1910   Tolstoy leaves his wife and is taken ill on the train. He dies on the platform of the Astapovo train station on November 7.

Contributors

HAROLD BLOOM, Sterling Professor of the Humanities at Yale University, is the author of *The Anxiety of Influence, Poetry and Repression,* and many other volumes of literary criticism. His forthcoming study, *Freud: Transference and Authority,* attempts a full-scale reading of all of Freud's major writings. A MacArthur Prize Fellow, he is general editor of five series of literary criticism published by Chelsea House. During 1987–88, he served as Charles Eliot Norton Professor of Poetry at Harvard University.

JOHN BAYLEY is Thomas Wharton Professor of English Literature at Oxford University. His books include *The Uses of Division, Romantic Survival, Shakespeare and Tragedy,* and *Pushkin: A Comparative Commentary.*

PAUL DEBRECZENY is Professor of Russian Literature at the University of North Carolina—Chapel Hill. He has translated and edited the complete prose works of Pushkin and a volume of nineteenth-century Russian literary criticism. His critical writings include *Nikolai Gogol and His Contemporary Critics* and *The Other Pushkin: A Study of Alexander Pushkin's Prose.*

ROBERT LOUIS JACKSON is Professor of Russian Literature at Yale University. He is the author of several books on Dostoevsky.

W. GARETH JONES has written several articles on Tolstoy.

EDWARD WASIOLEK is Avalon Foundation Distinguished Service Professor of Russian and Comparative Literature at the University of Chicago. His books include *Dostoevsky: The Major Fiction* and *Tolstoy's Major Fiction.*

PATRICIA CARDEN is Professor of Russian Literature at Cornell University.

MARTIN PRICE is Sterling Professor of English at Yale University. His books include *Swift's Rhetorical Art: A Study in Structure and Meaning, To the Palace of Wisdom: Studies in Order and Energy from Dryden to Blake*. He has also edited a number of volumes on literature of the seventeenth, eighteenth and nineteenth centuries.

Bibliography

Bayley, John. *Tolstoy and the Novel.* New York: Viking, 1966.

Berlin, Isaiah. *The Hedgehog and the Fox: An Essay on Tolstoy's View of History.* New York: Simon & Schuster, 1953.

Bidney, Martin. "Water, Movement, Roundness: The Epiphanic Pattern in Tolstoy's *War and Peace.*" *Texas Studies in Literature and Language* 23 (1981): 232–47.

Carden, Patricia. "Career in *War and Peace.*" *Ulbandus Review* 2, no. 2 (Fall 1982): 23–38.

———. "The Expressive Self in *War and Peace.*" *Canadian-American Slavic Studies* 12, no. 4 (Winter 1978): 519–34.

Christian, R. F. *Tolstoy: A Critical Edition.* Cambridge: Cambridge University Press, 1969.

———. *Tolstoy's* War and Peace: *A Study.* Oxford: Clarendon, 1962.

Cook, Albert. "The Moral Vision." In *The Meaning of Fiction.* Detroit: Wayne State University Press, 1960.

Crankshaw, Edward. *Tolstoy: The Making of a Novelist.* New York: Viking, 1974.

Dukas, Vytas and Glenn A. Sandstrom. "Taostic Patterns in *War and Peace.*" *Slavic and East European Journal* 14 (1970): 182–93.

Farrell, James T. *Literature and Morality.* New York: Vanguard, 1947.

Gibian, George. *Tolstoy and Shakespeare.* The Hague: Mouton, 1957.

Greenwood, E. B. "Tolstoy's Poetic Realism in *War and Peace.*" *Critical Quarterly* 2 (1969): 219–33.

Gunn, Elizabeth. *A Daring Coiffure.* London: Chatto & Windus, 1971.

Knowles, A. V. "War over *War and Peace:* Prince Andrei Bolkonsky and Critical Literature of the 1860s and Early 1870s." In *New Essays on Tolstoy,* edited by Malcolm V. Jones. Cambridge: Cambridge University Press, 1978.

———, ed. *Tolstoy: The Critical Heritage.* London: Routledge & Kegan Paul, 1978.

Lubbock, Percy. *The Craft of Fiction.* New York: Peter Smith, 1947.

Lukács, George. "Tolstoy and the Development of Realism." In *Studies in European Realism,* translated by Edith Bone. London: Hillway, 1950.

MacMaster, Robert E. "No Peace without War: Tolstoy's *War and Peace* as Cultural Criticism." In *American Contributions to the Eighth International Congress of Slavists, Zagreb and Ljublana, September 3–9, 1978,* vol. 2, edited by Victor Terras, 438–84. Columbus, Ohio: Slavica, 1978.

Mann, Thomas. *Goethe and Tolstoy.* Aachen, W. Ger.: K. Spiertz, 1923.

Matlaw, Ralph, ed. *Tolstoy: A Collection of Critical Essays*. Englewood Cliffs, N.J.: Prentice-Hall, 1967.

Merezhkovsky, D. S. *Tolstoy as Man and Artist, with an Essay on Dostoevsky*. London: Constable, 1902.

Morson, Gary Saul. "Tolstoy's Absolute Language." *Critical Inquiry* 7 (1981): 667–87.

Naumann, Marina T. "Tolstoyan Reflections in Hemingway: *War and Peace* and *For Whom the Bell Tolls*." *American Contributions to the Eighth International Congress of Slavists, Zagreb and Ljublana, September 3–9, 1978*, vol. 2, edited by Victor Terras, 550–69. Columbus, Ohio: Slavica, 1978.

Poggioli, Renato. *The Phoenix and the Spider*. Cambridge: Harvard University Press, 1957.

Rzhevsky, Nicholas. *Russian Literature and Ideology: Herzen, Dostoevsky, Leontiev, Tolstoy, Fadeyev*. Urbana: University of Illinois Press, 1983.

Sherman, David J. "Philosophical Dialogue and Tolstoy's *War and Peace*." *Slavic and East European Journal* 24 (1980): 14–24.

Simmons, Ernest J. *Introduction to Tolstoy's Writings*. Chicago: University of Chicago Press, 1968.

———. *Tolstoy*. London: Routledge & Kegan Paul, 1973.

Speirs, Logan. *Tolstoy and Chekhov*. Cambridge: Cambridge University Press, 1971.

Steiner, George. *Tolstoy or Dostoevsky: An Essay in the Old Criticism*. New York: Knopf, 1959.

Thale, Jerome. "*War and Peace*: The Art of Incoherence." *Essays in Criticism* 16 (1966): 398–415.

Wasiolek, Edward. "The Theory of History in *War and Peace*." *Midway* 9, no. 2 (Fall 1968): 117–35.

———. *Tolstoy's Major Fiction*. Chicago: University of Chicago Press, 1978.

Wilson, Edmund. "The Original of Tolstoy's *Natasha*." In *Classics and Commercials*. New York: Farrar, Straus, & Giroux, 1960.

Zweig, Stefan. *Master Builders: A Typology of the Spirit*. New York: Viking, 1939.

Acknowledgments

"Not a Novel . . .": *War and Peace* by John Bayley from *Tolstoy and the Novel* by John Bayley, © 1966 by John Bayley. Reprinted by permission of the author, Viking Press, Inc., and Chatto & Windus, Ltd.

"Freedom and Necessity: A Reconsideration of *War and Peace*" by Paul Debreczeny from *Papers on Language and Literature: A Journal for Scholars and Critics of Language and Literature* 7, no. 2 (Spring 1971), © 1971 by the Board of Trustees of Southern Illinois University. Reprinted by permission.

"The Second Birth of Pierre Bezukhov" by Robert Louis Jackson from *Canadian-American Slavic Studies* 12, no. 4 (Winter 1978), © 1978 by Charles Schlacks, Jr., and Arizona State University. Reprinted by permission.

"A Man Speaking to Men: The Narratives of *War and Peace*" by W. Gareth Jones from *New Essays on Tolstoy*, edited by Malcolm V. Jones, © 1978 by Cambridge University Press. Reprinted by permission of Cambridge University Press.

"*War and Peace*: The Theoretical Chapters" (originally entitled "*War and Peace*") by Edward Wasiolek from *Tolstoy's Major Fiction* by Edward Wasiolek, © 1978 by the University of Chicago. Reprinted by permission of the University of Chicago Press.

"The Recuperative Powers of Memory: Tolstoy's *War and Peace*" by Patricia Carden from *The Russian Novel from Pushkin to Pasternak*, edited by John Garrard, © 1983 by Yale University. Reprinted by permission of Yale University Press.

"Forms of Life and Death: *War and Peace*" by Martin Price from *Forms of Life: Character and Moral Imagination in the Novel* by Martin Price, © 1983 by Yale University. Reprinted by permission of Yale University Press.

Index

Account of Yesterday, An, 28
Akhsharumov, 91
Alexander, Emperor, 12, 46, 68, 71, 90, 95, 101, 123, 124
Alpatych, 33
Andrey. *See* Bolkonsky, Prince Andrey
Andreyev, Leonid Nikolayevich, 34
Anna Karenina, 29, 32, 33, 89, 102, 121
Anthropological Principle in Philosophy, The (Chernyshevsky), 43
Ardens, N. N., 45
Austerlitz, battle of, 19, 22, 46, 69, 70, 117, 125, 127

Bagration, Prince, 90, 98
Bayley, John, 50
Berlin, Isaiah, 3, 25, 44, 91–92, 94, 95, 96, 97, 100, 101–2
Bezukhov, Pierre, 1, 13, 29, 55–63, 69, 71, 121; and Andrey, 19, 109, 126, 127; and the executions, 14–17, 41, 42, 55–57; and free will, 48, 102; goodness of, 129–30; and Hélène, 48, 78, 129; intellectualism of, 52; and Natasha, 3–4, 10, 21, 84–86, 117, 128, 129–30; physical appearance of, 16–17, 18, 125; and Platon Karataev, 56, 57–59, 61–62, 130; sincerity of, 66–67, 79, 83; and Tolstoy's narrative technique, 14–17, 77, 78, 84–86
Big Two-Hearted River (Hemingway), 87
Bilibin, 71, 72, 76, 77–78
Blackmur, R. P., 52
Bocharov, 87, 88
Bolkonsky, Prince Andrey, 1, 3, 13, 18, 29, 33, 61, 130; death of, 22, 23–25, 27, 30–31, 116–21; and deception of narration, 67, 69–70, 83–84; detachment of, 21–22, 50–52, 118, 126–29; in earlier versions of *War and Peace*, 19, 46–47, 117–18; emotional

complexity of, 77–78, 79; and foreign languages in *War and Peace*, 71–73; and free will, 46–48, 49–50, 101, 102; and meeting with Natasha, 19–20, 47; and memory and immortality, 109, 118–21; military life of, 125–26, 128; and Pierre, 19, 109, 126, 127; and reaction to Natasha's infidelity, 23, 51–52, 118, 128, 129; and relationship with Natasha, 22, 75, 76, 78, 79–80, 82, 113, 127–28; and sky image, 88, 126, 127, 128; as symbolic figure, 19, 21
Bolkonsky, Prince Nikolay, 18, 38, 48, 116
Bolkonsky, Princess Elizabeth, 47, 48, 51
Bolkonsky, Princess Mary, 3, 4, 13, 83, 84, 116, 117, 119; and death of Andrey, 22, 23–25, 27; spirituality of, 120–21, 129
Boris. *See* Drubetskoy, Boris
Borodino, battle of, 22, 41, 55, 63, 73, 83, 84, 117, 121, 125, 128, 130
Bourrienne, Mlle., 17, 38
Boyhood, 19. *See also* Childhood, Boyhood and Youth
Brekhunov (*Master and Man*), 33, 34–35
Büchner, Ludwig, 43

Captain's Daughter, The (Pushkin), 11–12, 13–14, 16, 18
Characters: attitude toward death of, 26–27, 32–33, 55–56, 60; complexity of emotions of, 77–78, 79; consistency of nature and fate of, 21, 36; as part of history, 41–42, 45–47; as performers, 66–68, 77, 79, 80–81, 83–86; physical appearance of, 16–18; and role of families, 112, 116; Tolstoy's didactic use of, 11, 12, 14–17, 33; Tolstoy's family as models for, 104; types of, 18–19
Chernyshevsky, N. G., 43, 50

Childhood, Boyhood and Youth, 19, 37, 65, 75, 77, 102, 111; death in, 26–29; and falsity of art, 33, 67–68, 70, 74; as a novel, 27–29
Chirkov, N., 45–46
Christian, R. F., 43–44, 85
Claudel, Paul, 79
Commandant, the (*The Captain's Daughter*), 11–12, 14
Confession, A, 52
Cook, Albert, 46
Cossacks, The, 29, 62, 89
Courrière, C., 90, 91

Darwin, Charles, 43
David Copperfield (Dickens), 29
Davout, General, 56
Dead Souls (Gogol), 9
Death, 19–36; Andrey as symbol of, 19, 21; attitude toward, as reflection of character, 25–27; as awakening, 24, 107, 109–10, 118; characters' disbelief in own, 32–33, 55–56, 60; vs. egoism of life, 31–34, 60–62; horror of, 36, 56; metaphors for, 30–31; Tolstoy's fear of, 103–4. *See also* Memory
Death of Ivan Ilyich, The, 25, 27, 30, 31, 32, 33, 34, 37, 60
Denisov, Vasska, 33, 123
Determinism. *See* Freedom
Dickens, Charles, 2, 8–9, 29, 39, 72
Dimmler, 80, 82, 106, 111
Discovering Plato (Koyré), 106
Dobroliuboy, N. A., 43
Dolokhov, 13, 83
Dostoevsky, Fyodor, 2, 9, 38, 41–42, 52
Dron, 33
Drubetskoy, Boris, 23, 33–34, 45, 68, 76, 78, 80–81, 82, 117
Dr. Zhivago (Pasternak), 13

Eikhenbaum, Boris, 107

Family Happiness, 88, 89
"Few Words About *War and Peace*, A." *See* *Some Words About* War and Peace
First Love (Turgenev), 38
Freedom, 2, 41–53, 87–102; and consciousness, 43–44, 93, 96–97, 99–100; and criticism of philosophical chapters, 90–91; and divine justice, 41–42; in hunt scene, 87–90; and immediacy of life, 99–100, 101–2; and individual vs. historical action, 41–42,

45–47, 49, 87, 91–93, 98, 99–101; and intellect, 52–53; and moral responsibility, 41–45, 91–92; and multiple causes of events, 93–95, 97–99, 125; and necessity, 25, 47–50, 89–90, 101–2; vs. vitality, 50–52

Garnett translation, of *War and Peace*, 89, 91, 96
Georges, Mademoiselle, 83, 114
Goethe, Johann Wolfgang von, 108, 109
Gogol, Nikolay, 9
Goldenweiser, Alexander Alexandrovich, 9, 34
Grigory (*Childhood*), 71
Grinyov, Ensign (*The Captain's Daughter*), 14, 16

Hadji Murad, 2, 12, 29–31
Hemingway, Ernest, 87
Herder, Johann Gottfried, 106, 109–10, 119
House of the Dead (Dostoevsky), 9

Iliad (Homer), 1, 52
Immortality ode (Wordsworth), 110
Ivan Ilyich (*The Death of Ivan Ilyich*), 25, 30, 32, 33, 36, 37

James, Henry, 1–2, 4, 7, 9, 10, 11, 21

Karagina, Julie, 33–34, 78, 80–81, 82
Karamazov, Ivan (*The Brothers Karamazov*), 41
Karamzin, Nikolai Mikhailovich, 81, 110
Karataev, Platon, 16–17, 29, 33, 52, 76, 85, 98, 125, 130; and Pierre, 55, 56, 57–59, 61–63
Karenina, Anna (*Anna Karenina*), 38, 46
Karl Ivanich (*Childhood*), 70
Khlopov, Captain (*The Raid*), 67, 74
Koyré, Alexandre, 106
Kraft and Stoff (Büchner), 43
Kreutzer Sonata, The, 33
Kuragin, Anatole, 17, 19, 23, 45, 46, 128; and Natasha, 20, 48, 78, 82–83, 114
Kuragin, Hélène, 48, 71–72, 77, 78, 82, 129
Kuragin, Prince Hippolyte, 67, 71, 117
Kuragin, Prince Vassily, 66, 98, 101
Kutuzov, General M. I., 13, 51, 71, 72, 76, 116, 117, 126; and Tolstoy's view of history, 45, 90, 101, 124, 125
Kuzmich, Ivan (*The Captain's Daughter*), 12

Language. *See* Narrative
Lavrin, Janko, 90
Lavrushka, 73–74, 76
Levin (*Anna Karenina*), 89
Lev Tolstoy (Eikhenbaum), 107
Lise, 47, 48, 51
Lubbock, Percy, 8, 9, 39, 41, 87, 90
Lukács, George, 2, 3, 52

Marx, Karl, 25
Mary, Princess. *See* Bolkonsky, Princess
    Mary
Masha (*Family Happiness*), 88, 89
Master and Man, 33–36, 37, 89
Maude, Aylmer, 69
Maupassant, Guy de, 8
Memoirs of a Madman, The, 25
Memory, 103–21; and ideal forms, 114,
    118, 119–21; and immortality, 104–5,
    107, 109–10, 111, 118; and knowledge,
    106–7; and preexistence, 110–11; and
    unity of consciousness, 114–16. *See also*
    Death
Meno (Plato), 106
Mirsky, 33
Morio, Abbé, 66
Mortemart, Vicomte de, 66
Myshkin, Prince (*The Idiot*), 10

Nabokov, Vladimir, 20
Napoleon, 17, 66, 67, 68, 71, 72, 74,
    123–24, 130; and Andrey, 125–26; and
    Tolstoy's view of history, 45, 46, 50,
    90, 91, 101
Narrative, 65–86; and characters as
    performers, 66–68; and deception of
    words, 67–68, 70, 76–77; detail in,
    36–39; and didacticism, 31; of historical
    and military events, 68–70, 73–75;
    and impossibility of perfect
    communication, 65, 74, 76, 78–79,
    83–84, 89; moral commentary in,
    11–12; naturalness vs. conventionality
    in, 80–81, 84–86; role of music in,
    65–66, 74–76, 79–83; and Tolstoy's
    relationship to readers, 66, 85–86; use
    of foreign languages in, 70–73; as used
    to convey emotions, 77–84
Natalya Savishna (*Childhood*), 26–27, 29
Natasha. *See* Rostov, Countess Natasha
Nekhlyudov (*Childhood, Boyhood and
    Youth*), 19
Nekhlyudov (*Resurrection*), 38, 42
Nikita (*Master and Man*), 33, 34–35
Nikolay, Count. *See* Rostov, Count
    Nikolay

Nikolay, Prince. *See* Bolkonsky, Prince
    Nikolay
Nikolenka (*Childhood*), 67–68, 70, 74
Notes from Underground (Dostoevsky), 42
Nouvelle Héloise, La (Rousseau), 115–16
Novel form, 7–11; *Childhood, Boyhood and
    Youth* as example of, 27–29; in Russian
    literature, 8–9, 10–11; *War and Peace* as
    example of, 2–3, 8–10, 28–29, 52–53
Noyes, Alfred, 90, 91

Olenin (*The Cossacks*), 29, 62
Onegin, Eugene (*Eugene Onegin*), 19, 20–21
On the Eve (Turgenev), 31
On the Origin of Species (Darwin), 43
Organic Development of Man, The
    (Dobroliuboy), 43
Otradnoe, 47, 112, 113, 114

Paix et la Guerre, La (Proudhon), 52
Peter Ivanovich (*The Death of Ivan Ilyich*),
    37
Petrushka (*Master and Man*), 34
Phaedo (Plato), 107, 108
Pierre. *See* Bezukhov, Pierre
Plato, 62, 104–5, 107, 108, 109–10, 114,
    118, 120, 121
Polikushka, 33
Praskovya Fedorovna (*The Death of Ivan
    Ilyich*), 37
Proclus, 110, 111
Proudhon, Pierre Joseph, 52
Pugachev (*The Captain's Daughter*), 11, 13,
    14
Pushkin, Alexander, 9, 11, 13, 14, 19, 20,
    33, 43

Rahv, Philip, 2
Raid, The, 67, 74
Ramballe, Captain, 55, 84
Republic (Plato), 62
Resurrection, 33, 42
Rostov, Countess Natasha, 46, 71–72, 78,
    84, 88, 114, 121, 124; and Anatole
    Kuragin, 20, 48, 78, 82–83, 114; and
    Andrey, 19–20, 21, 22, 23–25, 47,
    51–52, 78, 80, 113, 127–28, 129; in
    earlier versions of *War and Peace*, 117,
    118; and free will, 48, 49, 98, 100, 101,
    102; and memory and immortality,
    105–6, 107, 108–9, 110, 111, 113, 116;
    and music, 39, 75–76, 79–80, 81–83,
    113, 128; and Pierre, 3–4, 10, 21,
    84–86, 129–30; as symbol of life, 19,
    20–21, 24–25, 26, 33, 52

Rostov, Count Ilya, 19, 25, 49, 88, 112
Rostov, Count Nikolay, 17, 52, 68, 102, 112, 123–24, 128; and battle of Schongraben, 32–33, 68–69, 83; and deception of narrative, 68–69, 70, 74, 76, 83; in hunt scene, 39, 89–90, 101; and memory and immortality, 105, 107, 109, 111, 113, 116; and Princess Mary, 13, 24, 117; and Sonya, 19, 78, 80, 88
Rostov, Count Peter, 29, 124
Rostov, Petya, 29, 124
Rousseau, Jean-Jacques, 108, 114–16
Russian Archive, 9
Russian Messenger, The, 8

Scherer, Anna, 45, 66, 67, 71, 78, 83, 85, 126; conventionality of, 98, 101
Schopenhauer, Arthur, 24, 107
Scott, Sir Walter, 13, 14, 18
Seeley, Frank F., 50–51
Sergey (*Family Happiness*), 88, 89
Shakespeare, William, 1–2, 5, 9, 13, 23
Shcherbatsky, Kitty (*Anna Karenina*), 89
Shestov, Lev, 24, 33
Shklovsky, Viktor, 81, 107–8
Snowstorm, The, 36
Socrates, 106, 107, 114, 119
Some Words about "War and Peace," 9, 13–14, 42, 72
Sonya, 20, 47, 48, 105, 110, 111; and Nikolay, 19, 78, 80, 88
Sorrows of Young Werther, The (Goethe), 108–9
Speransky, 90, 126, 127–28
Sportsman's Sketches, A (Turgenev), 11
Steiner, George, 52
Stendhal, 7, 8
Stiva (*Anna Karenina*), 33
Strider, 33

Tales of Army Life, 69
Tatiana (*Eugene Onegin*), 20–21, 112
Thiers, Louis-Adolphe, 73–74
"Three Deaths, The," 60, 61
Tolstoy, Leo: on art, 2, 5, 7, 9, 114; and family idyll theme, 112–14; on fictional characters, 21, 36; on form of *War and Peace*, 8–9; humanism of, 62–63; humor of, 33–34, 36; influences on, 1, 13, 24, 107–9, 114–16; intellectualism of, 52–53, 107–8; ironic detachment of, 81; moralism of, 16, 61; on novel form, 8–9, 27; Platonic influence on,

104–12; and preparation for writing *War and Peace*, 104; "primitivizing" of scenes by, 88–89; role of music in writings of, 65–66, 74–76, 79–83; on Russian literature, 8–9, 10–11; use of detail by, 36–39; use of foreign languages by, 70–73; use of repetition by, 85; on writing, 65, 103. *See also* Characters; Death; Freedom; Memory; Narrative
Turgenev, Ivan, 10–11, 31, 37, 38, 43, 52, 90
Tushin, 98, 109

Volodya (*Childhood*), 70
Vronsky (*Anna Karenina*), 46, 123

War and Peace: absurdity in, 56, 57; *Anna Karenina* compared with, 102, 121; anti-intellectualism of, 52–53; *Childhood, Boyhood and Youth* compared with, 28–29; coincidences in, 13; detail in, 36–39; early versions of, 8, 46–47, 117–18, 121; execution of French incendiarists in, 14–17, 41, 42, 55–63; family idyll in, 112–14; Garnett translation of, 89, 91, 96; hunt scene in, 39, 87–90; individual vs. historical in, 13–14, 41–42, 45–47, 87, 91–92, 98, 99–101; love affairs in, 78–84; metaphor in, 37–38, 120–21; as network of narratives, 3, 66; moral questions vs. ordinariness of life in, 57–62; music in, 74–76, 79–80, 81–83, 106; oak image in 21, 47, 48, 101, 127; reality vs. conventionality in, 84–86, 98; Russian vs. Western ways in, 79–80; simplicity of, 3–5, 11; sky image in, 88, 126, 127, 128, 130; story-telling in, 66–67; Tolstoy's preparation for writing of, 103–4. *See also individual characters*; Characters; Death; Freedom; Memory; Narrative; Novel form
What is Art?, 2, 7, 114
Winter Evening (Pushkin), 33
Wordsworth, William, 65, 85, 110
World as Will and Idea, The (Schopenhauer), 24

Yasnaya Polyana, 104, 109, 112–13
Youth, 19. *See also Childhood, Boyhood and Youth*